The Jacaranda Flower

Toril Brekke

The Jacaranda Flower
*and eleven other stories
from Africa*

Translated by Anne Born

Methuen

For
Kjellan and Florenz,
Alice, Judith, Esther and John,
Ase, Kuldip and Jorun.
And Jon.
And all the others who have
helped me along the way.

THE JACARANDA FLOWER

First published in Norway 1985
by Forlaget Oktober A/S, Oslo
First published in Great Britain 1987
by Methuen London Ltd
11 New Fetter Lane, London EC4P 4EE
Copyright © Toril Brekke, 1985
Translation copyright © Anne Born, 1987
Printed and bound in Great Britain
by Richard Clay Ltd, Bungay, Suffolk

British Library Cataloguing in Publication Data

Brekke, Toril
   The jacaranda flower: and eleven other
   stories from Africa.
   I. Title
   839.8'2374[F]   PT8950.B77/

   ISBN 0–413–14870–X
   ISBN 0–413–14880–7 Pbk

Contents

Preface

At the beginning of January 1985 Grethe Mathismoen rang me up from the Norad office and asked if I would like to go to Africa. To Kenya. Had I heard aright? Was someone offering to treat me to a trip to the continent I had never visited but for so long had dreamed of seeing?

My assignment was to write about village women. It would form part of a larger work* to be published by a London firm in connection with the United Nations Women's Conference in Nairobi held in July 1985. Ten women authors from ten different countries were to travel to ten other countries and write about various aspects of women's life.

The detailed information I received from England in defining my task focused on three problem areas:

1. Why do Kenyan women want so many children?
2. What are the particular problems of single women in villages?
3. Can it be an advantage for women to live without men?

The background was the high birth-rate among Kenyan women (an average of seven, one of the highest in the world) and the fact that an unusually large number of women in villages live alone with sole responsibility for children and housekeeping, because the men go to the towns to find work.

* *Women:A World Report*, Methuen London, 1985.

I arrived at the end of January and stayed for three weeks. With the generous help of the Norad office, the NRK office and the Norwegian Embassy in Nairobi, also the consulate at Mombasa, I was given ample opportunity to meet local people on their home ground; I stayed with an African family in a village near Kisumu, the third largest town in Kenya, for a week, and also made close contact with people from places like Muranga, in Kibuyuni, Kwale and Kiambu, Kikuyus and Luos, Diegos and people from the Kalendji tribe, Muslims and Christians. A striking impression of light and colour, taste and smell, everyday life and history, which put most of my preconceptions and attitudes to shame. An experience which taught me a lot.

Special thanks to Halle Jorn Hanssen and Grethe Mathismoen at the Norad office, who organized the assignment and provided me with background material and good advice all through.

Toril Brekke
Oslo, August 1985

With empty hands they come;
from one man's house
to another man's house;
they who bear the burdens

It was the Quaker's idea for us to go and see Rose's new house. We set off after the day's work at the weaving shop; the long-legged Quaker with his camera on a shoulder strap, Rose, Rachel and myself.

The path is narrow and we walk in single file, the sun burning our backs, while the Quaker tells us enthusiastically about his fellow believers back home who had recently sent him some money they wished to be given to a worthy cause. It had coincided with the birth of Rose's last child. He had visited her, and the sight of Rose in the run-down old house had prompted him to give her the money to build a new one. He had also helped her to buy materials and driven to Kisumu in his own car to get corrugated tin for the roof.

Rose walks ahead in silence. Even Rachel, usually laughing and talkative, goes along without a word. I have a kind of presentiment that all is not as it should be.

The nearer we get to Rose's place the slower she walks; even the sound of one of her children crying doesn't make her speed up. The Quaker, who is describing the corrupt headmaster of the school where he works, almost stumbles over her several times. This headmaster has embezzled a whole year's school funds and has bought a small bus, a matatu, which he drives people around in, earning money for himself and leaving the school in the lurch.

We have arrived. We have met the other women in the courtyard and Rose's children, who number eight aged between one month and fourteen years old. They stand huddled together, scared, just behind the white man with the camera. A few yards in front of us is Rose, alone in the dry grass. She is barefoot, dressed in her blue skirt and a short white blouse that I know has a long tear down the back. Her arms hang down at her sides, her fists clench and unclench, she looks at us, looks through us or past us with a gaze I can't read: rejecting? desperate?

She stands there straight and serious. On either side of her, thin tree trunks are stuck into the ground, twenty crooked tree trunks to mark out the square outlines of a future house, a skeleton with half a roof made of tin sheeting. Rose stands in the shadow of the roof, alone, facing the Quaker, her children, the other women, Rachel and me.

The white man clicks his camera. His cheerfulness from the walk has vanished; he looks at Rose in despair, takes yet another shot of her, says he won't come back before the house is finished, says it won't be long before he comes back anyway, and then he will take the tin sheets away from her if nothing more has been done. Then he makes a poor attempt at a smile as if to soften the harsh effect of his words.

Rose makes no reply. She walks out of the shadow, turns her back on the monstrosity of wood and tin, turns her back on us all and walks slowly towards her old house; a dilapidated round mud hut with a straw roof.

'You don't understand,' says Rachel.
   We're back on the path, the Quaker, Rachel and I.
   'But surely it's not so hard to build a house?' he asks.
   'Building a house is a man's job,' says Rachel.
   'Then her husband should build it, now he is back from town.'

'But he says he won't. When others have paid to get it started, they can finish it, he says.'

'Does he want his wife to live in a house that will collapse in the next rainy season?'

'You don't understand. . . .'

Reality is a dusty red track. Sisal plants. Thorn bushes. Rachel disappears into the thicket and comes out with a load of wood on her head.

People must be happy in this country, I'd thought, under the brightly-hued crowns of jacaranda and flamboyant, happy, I'd thought, with the taste of passion-fruit, pineapple juice and thirst-quenching coconut milk on my palate.

But ahead of me on the path walks Rachel, black and shining in the heat, in her red blouse and a yellow kanga round her waist, firewood on her head and a profile that tells me she is wondering how she can get these white people to grasp the meaning of the picture held on the film in the man's camera: the picture of Rose under the tin roof.

I've been staying with Rachel's family for four days. A large enclosure surrounded by mud huts and houses. The two oldest huts belong to the parents-in-law; he has had only one wife, now she lies in her hut at the point of death. Her husband wears blue overalls and a brown cap, spends his mornings working on the shamba. One of his daughters-in-law cooks for him. The old couple have had four children. The three daughters were married off and live elsewhere; John the son is a teacher in the town, he shares a small flat with his third wife, who is young and as yet childless. But at least once a week John comes home and sleeps with one of his other two wives, Rachel or Eleonorah. Eleonorah is his first wife; she is a teacher too, at a primary school close by. She has the best house in the group, square with three rooms and a proper floor. The roof is tin and not straw, and she has a gas cooker and a battery-operated television. I have been lent one of her rooms. Rachel, on the other hand, lives in mud huts: she has two, one for a kitchen and one for a bedroom.

I'm sitting in Rachel's kitchen-hut watching her prepare dinner. She is cooking spinach in a pan over an open fire right at the back of the hut. The cramped space is filled with smoke that stings the eyes, hens flap around our feet and a couple of goat-kids are here, too. I want to talk about Rose.

I think it's about men and women. About old traditions. About white and black.

I tell Rachel about a book I've read which described how, when they marry, African men have to build their wife a house. Perhaps Rose's husband has been upset by other people meddling with what is his responsibility?

Rachel sits on a stool with her legs apart, making ugali, a kind of maize porridge. She nods.

'A man's wife must live in a man's house,' she says.

I think about Rose's husband. About the mean huts his wives have to live in. He has three wives whose homes are equally wretched, huts full of cracks and blackened ceilings, about to fall apart. His little patch of ground is far too small to support such a large family. His children are dressed in rags, and all of them stay at home every day because there is no money for school uniforms and books. I think of Rose's husband who has been in Nairobi almost a year looking for work, and came home recently wearing the same clothes and with his pockets as empty as when he set out. Where had he lived in Nairobi? In Mathare Valley, where 150,000 people are crammed together in plank and cardboard shelters? I've been there; I've met seventeen-year-old Ann, a prostitute, and her mother who makes a meagre living out of selling bad liquor.

Rose's husband who has not once sent money home during the year he has been away. Was it because he had none to send?

Rose's husband who comes home to find the strange skeleton of a new house on his ground. On his own land. What other men were entitled to build on his land?

Is that the explanation?

Rachel nods again. That is what it's about. Among other things.

Her two-year-old son runs into the hut with tear-stained cheeks; the puppy has bitten his bare toes. But not hard, there's no mark to be seen, and in a minute or two it's forgotten.

'But why couldn't the Quaker understand all this?' I go on.

'He did it from kindness,' says Rachel. 'He is kind. I was with him when he went to congratulate Rose on her latest child. I can still see his face when he went into the hut and saw the terrible walls and roof. He didn't want Rose to live like that. And then he felt angry with a man who could let his wife live like that and had sent her neither letters nor money after he left. . . .'

Seventeen hundred charitable shillings. Twelve sheets of tin and twenty flimsy tree trunks. The beginnings of a house that would be six times as big as Rose's old hut; six times as big as those of her fellow wives. This has something to do with it too. And spending 1,700 shillings on tin when a pair of trousers for one of the children costs 30 shillings and there is no money for trousers. Or school uniforms. Or blankets for warmth at night in the rainy season. Or a cockerel or a bit of fish at least once every fortnight . . .

'You're beginning to understand,' says Rachel.

*

I sit in the doorway of my room and read VIVA, the Kenyan women's magazine. The lay-out is attractive and the headlines exactly similar to those in American, French or Norwegian magazines: 'Your guide to the premenstrual syndrome', 'The male menopause', 'Faithful husbands: do they exist?'.

Out in the yard big light-coloured speckled cows and little spotted goats were grazing. A hen settles to lay an egg under a wash bowl against the wall beside me. John comes home from town. He walks past Rachel's huts without a glance inside, turns the corner and goes up to Eleonorah's door. I think 'gas cooker', and wonder whether she bought something nice for him at the market on her way home from school.

I go on reading the article about faithful husbands. A strange article seen from my viewpoint in this doorway, because it's about fidelity to a purely monagamous marriage. I have, of course, met African men who have chosen to live with only one wife as a matter of principle. Like George in Nairobi. I was shown their wedding photographs: George and Ruth on the church steps, he wearing a black suit and she in white, their wedding cake a tall marzipan cake with a little bridal pair on top. It was so familiar that I didn't reflect on what I had seen until later. Christianity versus African traditions. And: how many Africans can afford black suits and lace dresses? And marzipan cakes?

Rachel comes bustling across the yard; her skirt flaps about her and she wears a flowered scarf round her head.

'What are you doing?'

'I'm reading about why African men are unfaithful.'

She stops in front of me, looks inquiring.

I pass her the magazine. She looks at the drawing

illustrating the article: a man sneaking home late at night, carrying his shoes. A classic European cartoon.

'What does it say?' asks Rachel.

'It's a lot of rubbish,' I say.

It's about man's quest for his dream-woman, one he may have met in his youth but never got. Perhaps he marries a woman who resembles her and then is disappointed, and continues to search for his dream-woman in others later on. It tells how the sexual needs of men are stronger than those of women; touches on personal hygiene, on how men whose wives are not particular enough will go to other women.

I look at Rachel and for some reason feel ashamed to have brought this magazine here, a Kenyan women's magazine that bears no relation to the Kenyan woman now facing me, a magazine from another world, my world more than hers, and it strikes me how far there is to go; for Rachel, for the elite women in Nairobi, for myself and my fellow sisters at home; a very long way to freedom and equality.

'Do you look down on African polygamy?' asks Rachel.

I shake my head.

'It's not like that with you?'

'It's forbidden to marry more than one woman at a time,' I say. 'But a lot of men have mistresses for short or long spells. And many married women have lovers.'

'And that works well?'

'No, it doesn't. It creates plenty of problems. Jealousy, divorce. . . .'

The first time I came across African polygamy was in Muranga, in the heart of Kikuyu country. The Kikuyu are the largest tribe in Kenya. Jomo Kenyatta was a Kikuyu.

Ruth and George took me there, to her parents. We drove out of the capital early one morning, through dry flat plains, through Thika with its enormous American-owned pineapple plantation, through colourful villages; a main street with pastel-coloured façades; a pink butcher's shop, a bright yellow milk bar, a small apple-green house with 'Hotel' painted over the door.

As we approach Mount Kenya the landscape grows greener and more fertile, full of small ridges and hills, cultivated fields, lively streams that sparkle in the sun.

When we arrive, Ruth's mother and brothers are in the tea plantation. With brisk hands they pick from row after row, throwing handfuls of fresh pale green shoots over their shoulders into the big baskets on their backs. There is a great contrast between the townsfolk and the tea-pickers: Mother Mable, barefoot and sweating, her sons in rough working clothes with knitted hats as protection from the sun, the husband who joins them with his scythe over his shoulder from pruning the coffee bushes, wearing black working trousers with light grey patches on knee and crotch; and Ruth and George, he in his well-pressed light summer suit and suede shoes and she in a charming sky-blue summer dress.

A happy reunion, smiles and handshakes.

An elderly woman is working alone at the other end of the plantation. When we go to lunch I ask George if she is going to join us. He laughs and replies in a low voice. No, she isn't. She is his father-in-law's first wife and lives alone in another house. At one time the two women and their children shared the work in the field, but they quarrelled so badly the husband divided the plantation in two. Two elderly women with half a field each. Two elderly women who rarely exchange a word.

*

Later I meet Esther in Kibera.

'How do you get on with your husband's first wife?' I ask.

'We're the best of friends,' Esther laughs. 'When my parents could not afford to go on sending me to school I asked my friend if she couldn't get her husband to marry me too, and he did . . . .'

I remember a television programme I saw in Norway in which an African woman defended polygamy. I quote her words to Rachel: 'In the West you try to hush up every form of infidelity. In Africa we're less hypocritical – a husband's women know about each other because everything is open.'

It's getting dark; we sit inside and light the lamp.

A lizard shoots across the wall. I hope it will eat the huge bee that flew in earlier in the day and disappeared up into the rafters.

'Perhaps we Africans are wrong to think everything is so much better in white society,' Rachel says slowly, 'but . . .'

We're having a cup of tea when someone knocks at the door. It's John and Eleonorah. He wears a dark suit with good shoes, she is in a smart red dress but barefoot. Is he going to greet Rachel, whom he hasn't seen for four days? Will they mind Rachel being here? Am I alone in thinking that Rachel's presence destroys the illusion of Mr and Mrs Johswa paying an evening call on the visiting European woman?

I fetch a plate of biscuits and a bowl of bananas and pour tea for everyone.

John is good-humoured and jovial, talks away, chiefly to me. His wives are silent. He talks about Kenya, the country's economy, foreign aid, the contrast between town and country, what do I think of Nairobi?

'A featureless city that could be anywhere.'

'How about Kisumu?'

Kisumu: 'Little Bombay' on the shores of Lake Victoria. Dominated by Indian commerce, Indian restaurants, shops, factories . . . I like Kisumu but wonder how Africans feel about Indian domination.

'They came here in 1904 to build the railway,' John explains.

He tells how the English transported labour from one colony to another, ships packed with Indian railway workers with one-way tickets. I am absorbed personally by the picture before me, the picture of the talkative, talented John with a wife each side of him. I try to imagine what it must be like to be John, to be Eleonorah, Rachel. . . .

'What about Mombasa?' asks John.

'Ah, Mombasa, pearl among cities . . .'

And I forget my private cogitations. I am in Mombasa, by Fort Jesus, in the street with market stalls on the pavements, in the ancient Arab quarter. John has been there too, and we exchange streets, buildings, images with mutual enthusiasm until I fall silent and let him go on alone. As I stop, I find myself on a roof overlooking the old harbour. Below me a group of youths lie on the grass smoking marijuana. Beyond them is the entrance to the covered stairway down which, in the old days, Arab slave-traders drove Africans into their ships.

Centuries of humiliation. Who had they become when their country was freed? Who are they now? When I ask Rachel about old songs and dances she shakes her head. Nairobi is full of breakdance. I'm struck by the fact that when women here talk about themselves they use the term 'the African woman', not 'the Luo woman' or 'the Kenyan woman'. I think of the fortuitous boundaries laid down by Europeans.

John talks of the long train journey from Kisumu to

Mombasa. The railway that binds the country together. . . .

Rachel sits in the shadows outside the cone of light from the small lamp. Silent. Rachel, who grew up a few miles further south. Rachel, who came here on foot with two empty hands to live with the man who had paid a bride-price for her. What does Rachel know about train travel, about Nairobi and Mombasa. . . .

John thanks me for the tea and gets up. I shake hands with them and we say goodnight. I go outside with them, stand there in the dark listening to the sounds in the trees, the grass. Above my head shines a white crescent moon.

As I get ready for bed, I hear Eleonorah moving about. She is on her own. I guess John has chosen his other wife tonight. I wonder: if Rachel had the choice, which would she prefer: a gas cooker or the nightly advances of her husband? And I wonder how much she earns from weaving? How long will she have to save up before she can afford her own cooker?

It was the Quaker who helped them start up the weaving project. Fifteen women who sit together a few hours every morning to weave belts. Beautiful patterns in red, blue, yellow, green. They have their own house with a terrace. The house was built with money the Quaker acquired from a foreign aid organization. It is on land belonging to John's family, close to Rachel's and Eleonorah's homes.

The women arrive about ten o'clock; each has already put in several hours' work on their shambas, making tea for the family, washing up and getting the bigger children off to school.

What they earn is based on how much they produce. Some work fast, some slowly. Some have to stop work for a while to go home and prepare lunch for the children who return in the lunch break. Others have fellow wives or mothers-in-law to take over some of their domestic chores.

The Quaker keeps a large ledger in which he records how many belts each woman makes. Once a month he goes to Nairobi with the finished goods. Then he returns with the proceeds.

'What do you spend the money on?' I ask Judith, one of the women in the group.

She's thirty-two and has had nine children. She became pregnant while still at school and married the child's father, who was already married.

'Lots of things . . . food, clothes, school uniforms,' she replies.

I ask how many of her children are at school.

'Four.'

Nine minus four, I calculate – and ask who looks after the five others while she is here.

'There are only three at home now. My first child was stillborn. The second died of smallpox when it was two weeks old.'

'Why have you had so many?' I ask.

'Do you think I wanted to? I'm ill every time I'm pregnant. And when the babies come I have no milk for them.'

'But doesn't your husband realize you shouldn't go through so many pregnancies when it makes you so ill?'

'It's a sign of wealth when a man has many children.'

'But if it makes you ill?'

'He doesn't know I'm ill.'

'But surely he notices?'

Judith ponders for a moment. Then she goes on:

'You see, the African woman never complains. At least not to her husband. A woman who complains is a bad woman. A sick woman also is a bad woman.'

She tells me about a friend who had three miscarriages. After that her husband sent her away.

'And who do you think wants her now?'

Mary is another of the weavers. She became pregnant at school too. I ask if she married the child's father.

Mary laughs and shakes her head: the father was her teacher.

'Why did you go to bed with him?'

Mary laughs again. Don't I know what men are like? When a teacher wants a female pupil what else can she do but submit? Besides, he'd let her stay on at school after her family could no longer afford the fees.

'What did he do when you became pregnant?' I ask.

'He expelled me.'

'But didn't he feel responsible?'

'He said he couldn't be sure he was the father. "Haven't you some other sponsors?"' he asked.

'And had you?'

Mary doesn't give a direct answer.

Instead she asks: 'Isn't it the same where you come from? Aren't many girls dependent on sugar daddies for their school fees?'

Sugar daddies. I recall a pink bus on the road in front of us when I was travelling from Muranga with George and Ruth. The windows of the bus were festooned with decorations and 'Sugar Daddy' was written on the rear window. I asked the others what the strange vehicle was and was met with giggling silence. At last George had explained: it was an organized tour for rich old men who paid young girls to join them.

'No,' I reply. 'No Norwegian girl is dependent on a sugar daddy to pay for her schooling. But many girls do sell themselves,' I add, 'for other reasons.'

Mary nods, apparently satisfied with my answer.

23

She is beautiful, sitting there in the early evening light; big brown eyes, full mouth and high cheek bones. Her hair is plaited in an intricate pattern with woollen thread intermingling with her black hair. I know it takes five or six hours to dress it like that, but then the coiffure lasts several months.

'What did your parents say when you became pregnant?'

'Nothing. What could they say? They couldn't afford the school fees, they knew the money had to come from somewhere. . . .'

Mary had married another man. He was already married and had no objection to her first child having another father.

'Did you love him?'

She laughs.

'Love him? Not to start with, maybe. After a while I grew fond of him. But not any longer . . .'

Mary is twenty-four. She has borne this man three children.

'Why not any longer?'

'He's not good to me. He drinks too much. Drinks away our money, what I earn from weaving. If I talk about it he treats me badly.'

'What does he do?'

'Don't white men ever beat their women?'

'Yes, they do.'

'I must tell Florenz that.'

'Why?'

'Because Florenz dreams about marrying a *mzungu*, a white man. She thinks white men are much kinder than African men. . . . What do you do when your men beat you?'

I tell her about our shelters for battered and raped women. But I also explain that this is something new and that many people still consider domestic violence a private matter and that women are ashamed to admit it, and hide it.

'They feel ashamed? The African woman never feels ashamed,' says Mary flatly. 'But there's nowhere for her to go.'

She tells me she once went to her mother-in-law for help. But her mother-in-law wouldn't believe her and told the husband. After that her husband beat her even harder for telling tales.

What goes on in a woman's hut concerns her and her husband only. No man allows his wife to tell others what goes on between them. . . . The only thing you can do is move. And that is the same as divorce . . . and a divorced woman is a bad woman. . . .

Mary is a single parent. Her husband has not lived at home for more than a year.

'Has he got a job?'

'I don't know.'

'Does he send you money?'

'No. The only thing he's sent since he left is a letter saying he's coming home in April . . . but I hope he stays away. That he'll find a job and send some money. He can come home just occasionally, then perhaps we could manage not to quarrel. . . .'

I lie on my stomach on the bed – it's where Eleonorah's daughters usually sleep – looking through my notes by the light of an oil lamp that belongs to the Quaker. I think about Judith and Mary; I think about what it must be like to go through nine pregnancies and nine births in fourteen or fifteen years. I recall my own three; the vomiting, the pelvis problems, small feet kicking at bladder and ribs, sleep broken by constant trips to the lavatory; but what if the lavatory is a hole in the ground, a latrine fifteen yards from the house? What if the house is a small round mud hut and the bed a single mattress you have to share with the children you already have – five, six, seven of them, and you and your swollen belly on a single mattress. . . . What if the mud hut is askew and full of cracks you vainly try to stuff with straw mats and bits of rag, like Rose's, and the world outside is crawling with puff adders and green mambas. . . .

Those are my thoughts when someone suddenly bangs on the door.

'*Karibu*,' I answer.

'*Karibu*,' Rachel repeats ironically, slipping inside. 'How could you know who was knocking? Is anyone welcome to come in when you're in bed?'

I get up, wrapping the blanket round my shoulders, and put the lamp on the table.

'You've forgotten again,' says Rachel. 'That's why I'm here.'

The shutters; I've forgotten the shutters again.

This is the second time she's come to warn me; the last time I excused myself by saying I'm used to curtains and not shutters, and that there is mosquito-netting between the window frames, and mosquitoes at least cannot get in, and the netting is thick and dark so it's difficult to see what's happening inside, and surely no strangers would come sneaking round the homes of Rachel and her family in the evening? Besides, I was just about to put out the light anyway. . . .

Now Rachel is closing the shutters.

'Why is it so important?' I ask curiously, convinced there must be a reason she is reluctant to tell me.

'What have you learned today?' asks Rachel.

'That African woman don't complain or gossip. And that they're good at keeping secrets.'

'Secrets?'

'Like why it's important to close the shutters at night?'
Rachel laughs.

'You whites are different from us,' she answers. 'There's a lot about Africa you can't understand. . . .'

'Such as?'

Rachel hesitates. Her expression is the same as it was in the market-place when I asked her if she thought I might ask for a picture of the witch doctor sitting on a blanket selling strange medicines. I try to coax her to open up by telling her about the Sami people or Laplanders in Norway. The Sami people? 'Yes, in Norway we have two tribes and the Sami are one of them – and they can do all kinds of strange things; they read the future in the palm of your hand, they brew wonderful herbal concoctions, and if I'm not mistaken, one of my ancestors was a Sami who could stop bleeding. . . . And they can cast spells.'

'What's that?'

'Cast spells on people.'

'With an evil eye?' asks Rachel.

'That too. And with the aid of thought.'

'Bewitch people with the evil eye. That's what happens here. Women suddenly bewitched, who run around at night naked, round and round, often several of them together. And if you look them in the eye you go mad.'

'So that's why you must close the shutters and lock the door?'

Rachel shudders, glances sideways at the dark corners.

I say, 'If I'd given birth to nine children in fourteen years, and worn myself out scraping together enough food and clothing for them, I think I might have needed a few nightly escapades too. . . .'

Rachel looks at me, offended at first, then she starts to laugh.

'It's nothing to laugh at,' she laughs.

'No,' I admit.

After she leaves I lock the door. Then I lie down and put out the lamp. Through the shutters I can hear the crickets singing. Then I fall asleep.

After a few hours I wake up. Has it started to rain? No, it is drums. And voices, some way away, rising and falling. Are the night witches coming? It is pitch black all around; I can't see a hand in front of me. I creep barefoot over to the door, open it and look out. The black African summer night is slashed by a bluish-white light some distance away. The wet grass in front of me is momentarily lit up, the trees beyond, the shamba behind the trees. Then all is dark again, until another blue-white light flashes across the sky. It seems to be coming from the same place as the drums and voices. Can it be fireworks? What are they drumming and shouting about? Am I right in thinking the sound is coming closer and closer? A cat rubs itself along my legs and startles me. The dogs at Eleonorah's door start to bark. Other dogs some way off answer them. Then the dogs are quiet again. I think: suppose I were a white settler's wife a century ago, here is a village in the middle of darkest Africa, black night all around, black night illuminated by blue light, black night filled with the sound of drums coming closer and closer. . . .

I go inside again, lock the door and pull the blanket over my head. I am no settler's wife. And I have read somewhere that African lightning is not necessarily followed by thunder and downpours. And the drums are definitely not coming closer, are they? I comfort myself with the thought that probably someone over there must have died. . . .

The next time I wake up it's four o'clock. Eleonorah's cockerel is crowing out of tune.

*

The morning is soft and mild. The big light-coloured cows with long horns graze among the houses, two speckled cocks chase each other around the yard, the puppy jumps up at Rachel's son and licks his face. The boy squeals joyfully, only half-afraid. Eleonorah has gone off to school. Rachel offers me tea, half a cup of tea and half a cup of milk with sugar.

The weaving group is holding a meeting today. They are going to discuss how to manage after the Quaker has gone. He's leaving in a couple of months.

'We have no business sense,' says Rachel.

'But you've been to school,' I say. 'You can add up?'

'Yes. But still.'

'What do you mean?'

'No Luo understands business.'

'Nonsense,' I object.

'It's not nonsense. The Kikuyu can do it. We can't. Many have tried, taken over some goods from an Indian in Kisumu; the goods were to be sold within a month, then you had to go back and settle up and get more goods. But when it's time to pay the Indian, there's no money to pay him with. Because there's always something you need – salt, sugar, flour – and then you dip into the money you have to keep for the month. The Kikuyu can do it. The Indians can do it. We can't.'

'The Luo in Kibuyuni can do it,' I say.

Kibuyuni: down at the coast, in the Kwale district not far from Mombasa. I tell Rachel about the women's group in Kibuyuni where Digo, Kamba, Taita, Duruma, Kikuyu and Luo have co-operated to improve conditions in the village. I tell her they keep hens, goats, money in the bank.

'When the bank account belongs to the group as a whole, no one can take money out for their own use,' I say.

And I tell her how the money eventually grew into a small shop, a maize mill, and a clinic.

Rachel nods thoughtfully. She pictures bank accounts and clinics. She has told me about her trip to Kisumu when she went there for her last confinement. On the way in she had gone by bus. One day after the birth, she had to leave hospital and walk the whole long way home with the baby on her back.

In Kibuyuni the women have a clinic just round the corner. They built it themselves and when the building was complete the authorities paid for equipment and the salaries of a doctor and a nurse.

I recall the pride of those women in a small village, pride in achieving something, pride in overcoming tribal differences of opinion, religious differences.

There are many such groups of women in Kenya. They start with modest savings. A proportion of their takings from the sale of vegetables and fruit goes into the communal account. The sale of eggs. Small tea kiosks. Roasted corncobs. Sometimes the aim is a large project like a well. It is traditionally the women's job to fetch water and many of them spend hours every day trudging with their heavy crocks of water under the blazing sun – carrying them on their heads according to Luo custom or on their backs, held by a strap around the forehead, in Kikuyu fashion.

'A clinic would be wonderful,' says Rachel.

It's almost ten o'clock and Judith and Rose come into the courtyard. Rachel gets out the key to the weaving room, and goes off with them to open the door. A few minutes later Sophie arrives. She sits down besides me on the ground, and leans against the wall of Rachel's kitchen-hut.

Sophie it twenty-eight, mother of five, heavy with

number six. She lives alone with sole responsibility for the children; her husband, like so many others, has moved into town to look for work.

I look at her worn face and think of the women's group in Kibuyuni which holds monthly meetings for new parents, runs discussions, and gives out free contraceptives. The authorities are indecisive over this question. Sometimes they advise smaller families and birth control, then come periods when the matter seems forgotten. At the moment the newspapers are full of the death of Minister Oliotipitip, who had thirteen wives and more than eighty children.

Man's pride, woman's burden. In the West we talk of the stronger versus the weaker sex. Here the women do all the carrying: water, firewood. I remember Mother Mable in Muranga. Mother Mable in the vast tea plantation. When her sons were not in school they helped her pick tea, but each evening when the big basket was filled with tightly packed tea, it was Mable who carried it. Sixty-year-old Mable, with up to forty kilos on her back, had to carry it two or three kilometres to the delivery point.

To my question on why the men can't do the carrying Rachel replied that the men's mothers would laugh at them. Their mothers would despise them and call them women.

I look at Sophie sitting on the grass in front of me and ask if she has anyone to help her now she is so heavily pregnant. She shakes her head.

'No co-wives?'

'No. There were two of us. But the other one took herself off a year ago. Three of her children went with her. The other two she left to me. . . .'

'What about your mother-in-law?'

'She doesn't help me. She's jealous of the money I earn

31

from weaving. She comes and borrows money from me
every week. Sometimes I can let her have some. But
usually I haven't any. We're only paid once a month.
And there's always so much to buy. . . . When I can't
spare her any money she says bad things about me, says
I'm mean.'

Sophie wipes her brow. She's sweating. A different
kind of sweat, one that doesn't come from the sun. Is she
ill? Is the child about to be born? I ask her and the
answer is a grimace. She gives me a meaning look.

'My husband's been home recently,' she says.

I don't understand. What does her husband's visit
have to do with her sitting here sweating and in pain?
Sophie won't tell me any more. She gets on her feet with
an effort and walks stiffly over to where the others are
sitting weaving on the terrace.

I picture the courtyard, surrounded by huts and houses.
The drainpipe that carries the water from Eleonorah's
roof and down into a large barrel in the rainy season. The
violet flowers of the jacaranda bush. The sedate cattle.
The old man in his brown cap in the background. Two
women in the foreground.

Sophie and Rachel. One big with child and sway-
backed. The other graceful and lithe. She gesticulates,
strokes her friend's arm; they come back together, go into
Rachel's sleeping-hut together. After a few minutes they
appear again, Sophie is holding a small bundle. They're
speaking a language I can't understand, Rachel holds one
of Sophie's hands in both of hers. She lets go of her and
Sophie leaves. Out between Rachel's two huts she goes,
slowly down the dry red road.

So many stories.

Rachel stands before me washing clothes. Trousers

and shirts, underpants and vests. They belong to the Quaker; he pays her to do his washing. I offer to help but she says, no, thank you. It's her job.

She works quickly with small quick movements. Talks in a low angry voice.

Men in bars. African men of all ages, side by side on bar stools, at small tables covered with bottles and glasses. Men digging deep in their pockets for a few more shillings, money that changes hands, money exchanged for beer and spirits. Loud-mouthed men. Men with hungry eyes, indifferent eyes, nonchalant eyes turned on the few women in the bar, women who have left their men, women who have been driven out, prostituted.

Men on their way home in the dark. Men stumbling into their huts to their wives, stumbling over sleeping children, throwing themselves on the women they own who have what they want. Does she refuse him? Does she dare say no?

'That's how it is,' says Rachel. 'D'you remember we talked about circumcision the other day? The Luo have never practised it. You know that. But what difference does that make when it's all a question of fear? The fear of yet another pregnancy. The fear of illness. The men do as they like. They go to anyone they set eyes on. A man can have two, three, four wives, but if he feels like it, he can still go to other women. We live in the man's hut. He owns the hut. He owns us. When my sister was widowed her husband's brothers emptied the hut of everything. Since their brother was dead they claimed everything belonged to them. . . . You ask me about love? Look at Sophie; she was one of the cleverest girls in school. She wanted to go on – to get somewhere. But girls can't get on if a man wants them and offers to pay the bride-price

33

and their father needs the money. Now Sophie's husband has lived in town and worked in a restaurant for more than two years. He's been back to see her twice in that time. The first time he made her pregnant again. The second time he made her ill. . . .'

Rachel rinses the Quaker's clothes and hangs them out to dry on some bushes. I wonder if African women cry.

Sophie, Judith, Mary, Rose, Rachel. I'm leaving them there, but I'll never forget them. I leave just a few hours before they hold their group meeting. On my way to Kisumu I imagine the meeting; sitting beside the pool at the Sunset Hotel, waiting for the train, I think up the questions and answers. What difference will it make when the Quaker leaves? They will go on weaving belts, expand their production to small kofias and vests, and the girls themselves will take the train to Nairobi and trade with Undogo and the other shopkeepers. Later on they will send their goods by post each month and when the money comes it will go straight into their newly opened account.

On the night train back to Nairobi I dream of them on the terrace, bent over the coloured yarn. Deft hands at work. The pride of knowing they can manage it all, that everything's working out. . . .

I dream Sophie is well again. That Rachel has a new gas cooker. I dream of Rose's children on their way to school in new uniforms, with books under their arms.

But Rose's house, that will never be finished.

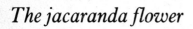

The jacaranda flower

Their names are Raymond and Ursula.

From my seat in the Delaware restaurant on Harry Thuku Road in Nairobi, I watch them crossing the road from the university. He wears jeans and a red shirt, she's in a sky-blue dress. I wave to them and Ursula waves back. In a moment or two they're sitting at my table. I ask if they're hungry but they shake their heads. We each order a glass of fruit juice, pineapple for me, orange for the others.

I was introduced to them through a mutual friend. Ursula has invited me to visit her family; when we have finished our drinks we're going to drive out to Kiambu.

They tell me about their life at university; her subject is mathematics, his languages.

'Which languages?'

'English and Spanish. Later on I want to do Arabic.'

The Kenyans are good at languages. I have met quite small children who can master both Swahili and English as well as their tribal language.

Raymond is full of enthusiasm about the Nairobi library; there were very few books at home in his village.

'He loves reading,' says Ursula.

They look at each other and smile. Two young people in their early twenties. They have known each other from childhood and decided to get engaged when they came to university. But they'll wait to get married until they've finished their studies.

'A Christian marriage,' says Raymond.

By that he means that he'll have only Ursula. One wife. Ursula lowers her eyes shyly.

'I want to move with the times,' he says; 'one wife and not too many children. Three perhaps. Or four. Who will look like Ursula. . . .'

She laughs, embarrassed. I look at her lovely clean-cut face. The delicately curved mouth. The almond eyes. Black hair twisted into a pony tail. And Raymond's boyish pride when he talks of her.

I ask how their studies are financed.

'We have state scholarships,' he says. 'Our families pay the rest. Parents, brothers, uncles. . . . When we've finished they'll expect us to help when other members of the family want to study later on.'

'My parents have problems,' Ursula tells me. 'I had a brother who gave me a lot but he has just married again and can't pay any more for a while.'

'She works in a restaurant three afternoons a week,' says Raymond.

'And Raymond helps me a bit,' she puts in.

They tell me their dreams; they want to travel, see other countries – Europe, America – perhaps he can find work as a translator, and she, who is a realist . . .

'Ursula is clever,' says Raymond.

We've finished our drinks, it's time to start for Kiambu. I have hired a Datsun, a yellow car with a big dent in its front bumper. I get in and start up while the young people say goodbye behind me. When Ursula gets in she's holding a purple jacaranda flower. We wave to Raymond. In the mirror I can see him standing on the pavement for a few moments watching us drive away before he crosses the road to go back to the university. Back to English and French. And Arabic later on perhaps.

We drive out of town. Open the windows to make a

draught so as not to suffocate with the heat. Tall leafy trees grow beside the road. Ursula is quiet, she caresses the flower on her lap. I think about love. The feeling of commitment. Being proud of each other.

Women and children walk along the road carrying heavy loads of wood on their backs. We pass big farms with long avenues leading to the main buildings. We pass little shanty towns for farm workers on the slopes that run down to the road.

After half an hour's drive Ursula tells me to turn off; along a narrow, bumpy earth track with thick bushes on each side.

Soon we've arrived.

A little courtyard with five or six huts around it. A woman enters it just as we do; she has come straight from the shamba and has a big knife in her hand. She and Ursula greet each other, I am introduced, shake hands with the woman who is Ursula's stepmother. Then we go over to the hut where Ursula's real mother lives.

She is lying down. She is not well. She gets up laboriously, looks me over and talks quietly to her daughter in a language I can't understand. I sense conflict in the air. Is her mother angry because Ursula has brought a visitor unannounced? I wonder if it's the right moment to bring out the box of sweets I've brought for the family.

They talk on for a while without heeding me. From her tone of voice I sense the daughter's respect for her mother, but she seems to be making objections to what her mother says. In the end they stop talking and the mother offers me her hand.

'*Jambo.*'

'*Jambo*,' I say in my limited Swahili.

Ursula tells me she has to go off somewhere. She has to visit someone; she doesn't know why, but her mother says she must. I can stay in her mother's hut while she is gone. She promises to be quick.

Ursula disappears among the trees; her mother puts out a stool for me. Then she goes out as well and comes back with a pineapple. She sits in the doorway and peels it. Then she puts the slices on a small tin plate and offers me some. I get out the box of sweets.

'*Asante sana*,' the mother says. I realize she knows very little English. I try to make conversation but she shakes her head, throws out her hands and offers me more pineapple.

We sit in silence. The other woman walks by, knife in hand and with a small child at her heels. The two women exchange a word or two.

We sit a while longer.

'Ursula?' I ask when an hour has passed.

The other shrugs her shoulders.

I go over to the car to fetch the cigarettes I've left on the dashboard. The jacaranda flower is on Ursula's seat. I go back, and light a cigarette; the older woman asks me something I don't understand, then she smiles for the first time and lights a little fire in the hut. She's making tea.

We drink the tea and smile helplessly at each other and outside dusk begins to fall.

After yet another hour of waiting a man arrives. I guess he's Ursula's father. He looks at me in surprise, greets me pleasantly and listens to his wife's explanation. His face gets serious, almost irritated.

He turns towards me and says, 'There's no point in waiting.'

'Why not?' I ask.

'She's not coming back.'

'Why not?'

He looks ill at ease, doesn't answer. He goes out, over to his other wife's hut.

I look at Ursula's mother but cannot make out her expression in the darkness of the hut. She is stoking the fire. I gather she is about to prepare a meal.

I get up from the stool. Put the cigarettes in my bag. Take a few steps towards the other hut where the man went. He comes out again, walks over to the car and runs his hand over it.

'I am sorry,' he says.

Then he shakes my hand in farewell.

I get slowly into the car. Drive slowly out of the little courtyard.

Next day I find Raymond and tell him what happened at Kiambu. His big black eyes open wide; he doesn't like what I tell him.

I have kept on the dented yellow Datsun; he asks to borrow it; he wants to drive out to see what's happened.

He comes back late that evening. His face is stiff and grey.

'I don't usually drink,' he says.

We find a small table at the edge of the bar area in my hotel. I order a Campari for myself and a whisky for him. He empties his glass and beckons for another. His hands shake a little.

'I have lost her,' says Raymond.

His voice is so low I can hardly hear his words.

'I have lost her. . . .'

He bends forward, holds his head in his hands. I wait patiently, ask no questions. My eyes move over the neighbouring tables; African women in beautiful clothes, African men, European, Asian men. A yard to two away from us is a little pool full of shining red fish.

'They have married her off,' says Raymond.

Someone bursts out laughing at the next table.

Ursula's father has married her off to a man she does not know, a man she does not want. It was to this man she had gone the day before. Without knowing why.

'And when she arrived there, they told her. That he had paid the bride-price, that she belonged to him.'

Perhaps she tried to run away from him, run back to her parents. . . . Perhaps he took hold of her, beat her, Raymond sees it all happening, shares it with me. The story of how his sweetheart is kept prisoner, raped again and again until the man is sure she is pregnant.

He orders yet another drink. He is angry and desperately upset. It is midnight before we get up to leave; he through the night to his lodgings, I to my hotel toom.

Next morning I go out to return the hired car. On the seat beside me lies the jacaranda flower. It is withered and dry.

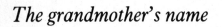

The grandmother's name

Gloria's stomach is as big and round as a ballroom. For almost nine months she's talked to it, talked to what's inside there under her skin. 'Hallo there, little boyo,' she's said again and again. But her stomach looks and feels just the same as it did the other times. And they were girls.

Gloria thinks the child should have been born several days ago, but she's held it back. It mustn't be another girl.

She is alone. The room's walls are painted bright blue, and it's crammed with furniture; a sofa along each of three walls and two or three deep armchairs with white loose covers; small tables with lace cloths; shelves, cupboards, a television set. It is on, but without the sound. Gloria sits in one of the deep armchairs and watches the little man who advertises Vaseline, every child's best friend.

But her thoughts are in Mururi. With her mother-in-law in her little house, with Lucy, mother-in-law's mother, who lives in the next hut. Old Lucy who pokes Gloria in the stomach and asks when 'the Lucy-child' will come.

They were there yesterday, in Mururi. Harry and herself and the girls, with Jackeline from the Ford Foundation and Washington DC.

'A trip like that will do you good,' Harry had said, 'We'll be home again by evening and then the baby's sure to come, don't you worry.' And sure enough she had felt something happening in her womb after they had gone to bed last night, but she'd kept it back. She'd closed her eyes and pretended to be asleep, held herself in. Then it had passed off.

The trip to Mururi: Harry behind the wheel of the embassy car; Jackeline, the children and herself in the back seat. Jackeline: all enthusiasm, full of questions, who laughed and commented and lit fresh cigarettes the whole time. Harry in his smart, light-coloured summer suit, happy, chuffed with the unexpected day off, with Jackeline, with the trip home to Mother in Mururi. Jackeline, who made them stop at the first market-place they came to because she wanted to get out and buy everything she had never seen before; Harry, who had been gallant and open-handed, loading her arms with breadfruit and mango, passion fruit and bananas.

Jackeline, who wanted to go to a milk bar but didn't like the milk because it was too thick.

'You must come and visit with me at home,' she'd said, 'then you'll get milkshakes. Strawberry milkshakes. Chocolate milkshakes . . .'

Visit Jackeline in America? She's not the first to invite them. After Harry got the job at the embassy they have met a lot of people who talk like that. People the ambassador asks Harry to take out to see his mother in Mururi, who repay him with a 'Come to America!' 'Come and visit us in New York.' They don't give a thought to the flight over the sea. They say it just to be friendly.

Wonder if Jackeline has a poor elderly mother living in the country several hours' drive from Washington DC they could go out to visit? And an even older grandmother, aged and sour, with a laugh like a cackling bird, and skinny pointed fingers, like Lucy. . . .

Oh yeah. That'd be something. Oh yeah.

It's Harry who talks like that. He talks quite

differently since he started this job. And his voice. And his eyes when he looks at her. Happy eyes. Harry is dishy.

Gloria isn't feeling so good. She's slumped in the armchair with her feet on a little stool. A yellow teacup balances on her stomach. She's tired; after the trip the day before, after she'd cleaned through all four rooms today, washed and tidied up and put everything in order for the others while she is in hospital.

Gloria strokes her stomach, presses it hard, but no little hand or foot responds to the pressure. She takes a deep breath and feels a faint movement.

'How many children do you want?' Jackeline asked yesterday.

How many children? Jackeline's questioning eyes above the girls' heads, Harry's smooth neck in the front seat, waiting for her answer. How many children. . . . Should she answer for Harry or for herself? Should she answer for Lucy or for her father or for the teacher who had discussed family planning with them?

'Are you asking my personal opinion?' she had said. And then she had told Jackeline about the naming-after tradition. The first son must be named after the paternal grandfather. The next after the maternal grandfather. The third after the paternal great-grandfather . . .

Jackeline had patted the girls' cheeks, calling them 'mother's mother's girl' and 'father's mother's girl'. She had held Marilyn, the youngest, on her lap for a while, admired her bracelet with the little blue flowers that had been a birthday present from the ambassador's wife, held her soft round fists and sung a song about a little bear.

*

The sun is sinking. Gloria looks away from the television screen; the Vaseline man has long since made way for first the shoe advert, then the jeans advert and now a news bulletin. Gloria raises her eyes to the window in the back wall and sees the trees are now black silhouettes against a purple sky. The child will be born tonight. A shudder runs through her body. She feels Lucy's fingers on her stomach.

Lucy, who suddenly put her head round Harry's mother's door and crinkled her little inquisitive eyes at them; was it yet another visiting American, yet another white female travelling the world and looking around her. . . ?

Mother-in-law, herself and Jackeline in the poorly lit room. The rickety low table. The dented tin plate. Milky tea. Pineapple and mango. The rusty red curtain hiding the bed in the corner. The photographs on the wall! Harry's parents on the little bench outside the house. Harry's mother inside, with two white women. 'God bless, from Mrs Mendelsohn.'

Jackeline asking question after question, and then suddenly Lucy, a dark silhouette in the doorway.

'How does your day go?' Jackeline had asked Harry's mother.

How big is your field? Which tribes live in Mururi? Does this tribe practise circumcision for women. . . ?

Lucy went away. And the room seemed lighter.

'White folk think they can come and ask questions about whatever they like,' came in Lucy's scornful tones in Kikuyu from outside. Harry laughed sombrely at her words. He respects his grandmother. Harry's mother and Lucy's daughter fingered her teacup nervously.

'Every girl-child was circumcised at one time,' she said in a low voice. 'But not any longer.'

'Were you?' Jackeline asked Gloria.

She shook her head.

'What about Harry's sisters?'

'Some were and some weren't. . . .'

It was late afternoon when they set off for home.

On the way they were held up by a funeral; hundreds of people on and beside the road, brass bands, cars. Harry tried in vain to push his way through by sounding the horn, but at the sight of a minister he gave up, and stopped the car, moved and curious.

They were delayed almost an hour. The dead man had taken part in the fight for liberation. The girls drank Pepsi and admired the shining musical instruments.

When they were at last able to go on, the children were asleep and it was almost dark. Gloria looked at Jackeline; at the orange glow from her cigarette, the eager inquiring eyes. Of course she has to ask questions and find out about things, Gloria thought – if I were in America I'm sure I'd want to ask about everything too, and not only about things the Americans thought ought to concern me . . . though it wasn't likely that Gloria would ever get to America.

She invited Jackeline in to tea after the trip. Partly because of the visit to Mururi. Because of mother-in-law's little house. The broken plastic plates. Old Lucy . . . Gloria wanted to show Jackeline from the Ford Foundation and Washington DC something else; a little brick house with proper glass windows, light rooms with modern furniture. Teacups without chips in them.

Harry put the children to bed. Gloria boiled water for tea. Jackeline sat on a sofa with white loose covers, her expression thoughtful, blowing grey smoke over the room. Harry went round to the neighbours with a message. Gloria put out cups and ashtrays, poured out the tea and milk and asked if her guest took sugar.

'Why are some girls in a family circumcised and others not?' asked Jackeline, looking puzzled.

Lucy's harsh voice rang in Gloria's ears.

She sank into the armchair and realized how tired she was.

'Why is that?'

Gloria stood up again, and remembered Jackeline hadn't replied to her question about sugar.

'You know. You said that some of Harry's sisters . . .'

'It's because of the traditions,' Gloria answered. 'Of who you are named after . . . the one the child is named after can decide. Our two girls were not circumcised because neither Harry's mother nor mine wanted it, but the third girl will be named after great-grandmother. . . .'

Gloria doesn't want to think about it. She has lighted the lamp. She has switched off the television. Been in to look at the children, and packed the small bag with the things she wants for the clinic.

Now she's back in her place in the deep armchair with her feet on the stool. Someone kicks her in the stomach. New bulges come and go on her flower-patterned dress. 'Hallo, there, little boyo,' whispers Gloria. The pains are regular now, Harry had better come soon if he wants the child born in hospital. The Lucy-child. . . .

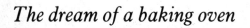

The dream of a baking oven

The interpreter provided by the Tototo Centre doesn't in the least wish to be my interpreter. Sullen and silent, she walks in front of me along the path, chewing gum and swinging her handbag. Have I done anything wrong? In Mombasa yesterday, when we planned the trip, she was all out to please. But not today, in the car from the town and here on the path. I wonder if I should feel guilty at bringing her out here but then recall that it's Mary Musangi who brought me and not the other way round.

She looks out of place in these surroundings; in a poppy-red wide-skirted dress with a broad yellow belt round her waist, high-heeled shoes and brandy-coloured tights. A glowing ship in contrast to the dry yellowish-green landscape.

We have walked for a quarter of an hour since leaving the main road. The sun is at its zenith and clothes stick to the body. I dream of ice-cold lakes.

'What is it you want to ask them about?' my interpreter snaps at me over her shoulder.

I don't answer. She knows that as well as I do.

The area we're walking in is an old white settler district the Africans have taken over. There is a women's group here, I am going to talk to the members about the group's activities. The path divides; we glimpse a house among the trees, and Mary Musangi goes towards it. It's a single-storey house with a veranda, whose roof is held up by pillars. The woodwork is unpainted and rotten, the veranda covered with rubbish; lengths of wood, cardboard, an overturned stool with one leg missing. The windows are blank, black holes without glass or netting. A woman in a thick pink wool jacket sits on a bench against the wall. She sits unmoving, it's like a photograph; the shabby house, the black windows, the woman like a pink patch against the wall. She sits with her legs apart, her hands in her lap; the only sign of life is her eyes, which follow us all the way across the yard in front of the house until we stop before her.

Mary Musangi says something in Swahili. They shake hands. The woman gets up, shakes my hand as well and goes into the house. She comes out again with two stools and a crying baby. We sit down. She puts the child to her breast.

'Go ahead and ask questions,' my interpreter says, cleaning her nails with a little twig, 'about anything you like. . . .'

'Is she a member of the women's group?' I ask.

She is. With thirty-eight others.

We're told how they grow onions, maize, tomatoes, potatoes as a communal enterprise. For sale. They have 1,000 shillings in the bank. The plan is a bakery. At present each member pays two shillings a week into the common fund; money they earn selling produce from their own plots. They may run a tea kiosk too; near the school, so that teachers and pupils can get tea in their free periods. A small baking oven costs 3–4,000 shillings. With it they can bake three hundred loaves a day.

The woman in the pink jacket talks slowly and monotonously. When Mary Musangi translates, it sounds as if she is making fun of the other woman. In the interpreter's words 300 loaves becomes an incredible amount; far too much in relation to the market. And

3–4,000 shillings an unattainable goal. Not to speak of the tea kiosk by the school; how many of the poor children here have any shillings in their ragged pockets to buy tea with. . . ?

The baby has emptied its mother's breasts. It's a little girl in a lace dress. She has a pearl necklace. Now she turns her head, catches sight of me and starts to cry again.

'She's not used to white people,' says Mary Musangi with a resigned look.

I feel I'm being watched: by eyes from the darkness behind the empty windowpanes or by glances hanging in the air; from among the leaves of the bushes or by the house corners. Suddenly another person is with us: a thin little woman in floppy black clothes she hides pineapples in. Hey presto! She's put a pineapple on the wooden boards of the veranda floor. Hey presto! There's another one. And she has more under her clothes. Without a word she conjures up a long sharp curved knife and begins to peel the fruit. The skin falls on the ground in long strips. The juice runs down over her hands and the knife; the sweet smell attracts small wasps.

We take big bites of pineapple, dribbling and waving away the insects with our free hands. The baby sleeps. When we have finished the fruit the silent woman vanishes as soundlessly as she came.

The two of them are co-wives. The eldest is childless.

'A shame,' says the interpreter of her own accord. She throws me a brief expressionless look.

'How many have you?' I ask her.

'This one has nine,' says Mary Musangi, meaning the woman in pink, 'that's the average,' she puts in briskly, before the mother of nine starts to count up all their ages, from twenty-one downwards.

I ask about the father. He lives in Mombasa. He has a job in a repair shop.

'Do you want to see the house?' asks my interpreter, after conferring with the other in Swahili.

We go into a dark corridor leading right through the house. Like the veranda it is crowded with old materials and rubbish. I am shown the children's bedroom. Three beds with tattered rubber mattresses. A cord hangs from the ceiling across the room, with clothes draped over it. Not to dry, but instead of a cupboard. A pile of newspapers fills one corner. I am shown the mother's room; a large bed in the middle of the room with a small cot by the wall. Crammed cardboard boxes on the floor. Sheets of cardboard covering half the window. The third and last room belongs to the first wife.

We leave the house on the other side and find more houses; a kitchen house with one end walled off for chicken and ducks. Behind the kitchen house is a wash-room made of rush mats and a latrine. Under a roof made of straw, seven or eight goats are tethered.

When Mary Musangi and I take leave of the woman she's sitting there just as when we arrived; in her pink woollen jacket, with her hands in her lap, she looks stuck fast to the shabby wall. She is probably one of the more well-to-do people in the district.

We walk on under the sun; my interpreter in front in her red dress, her bag over her shoulder. We go past a small cultivated field. Then the bush grows thick again on both sides of the path. Then it opens out again; small bushes with cotton on the twigs. Mary Musangi groans with the heat, I refrain from asking what the cotton bushes are called so as not to irritate her unnecessarily. Her forehead glistens. She trudges along the bumpy path. I wonder why she doesn't take more care of her shoes and brandy-coloured tights.

Next we visit the first leader of the women's group, an old grandmother who sits in a yard surrounded by a crowd of undernourished grandchildren. With glowing eyes she talks about the baking oven they will have, the oven that will produce 300 fresh loaves a day, bread to sell to neighbours, to people all over the district; maybe they'll make an arrangement with a restaurant or a hotel in town . . . the oven that will bring profit, money, fresh bread, meat and fish to the listless youngsters around her, bring back the shine to the dry reddish hair, make them run around and play instead of drooping against each other, staring at chance strangers with big thoughtful eyes.

As we walk away the old woman shouts at my interpreter to come back; she's gone into the house, she has something to give her. It is a little root. She gives it to Mary Musangi after noticing a small swelling on one of Mary's wrists. Mary must do this and that with the root and the swelling and then it will be cured.

My interpreter gives me an inscrutable look as she puts the root in her bag.

In the shade of some big trees a young woman stands and shakes mats outside a little house. In the doorway close to her head hovers a dense swarm of mosquitoes. The strange woman greets us with a smile and goes on shaking her mats.

She is a member of the women's group too, says Mary Musangi. But she hasn't any land, so she's had problems contributing to the savings fund every week. So on her own initiative she started a playgroup. At the moment the children are at home for lunch.

'How many children?' I ask.

My interpreter translates.

'Thirty-six.'

'Just you, all on your own?'

'Yes. Just her.'

'And how much can you earn from that?'

Mary Musangi laughs. Both women laugh. My question goes unanswered.

'She says, when they get the oven they'll be able to afford to pay her,' says Mary Musangi, through her laughter.

It's cool and shady under the tall tree crowns. As if enchanted. A strange heavy stillness. Not a leaf rustles. Not a dry twig snaps. Nothing until another house or a hut appears behind the leaves and great black tree trunks.

Two sleeping children, side by side on a rush mat on the ground. A woman putting her washing out to dry on the withered grass. A wash made up of shabby clothes full of holes that have to be dried by the warm air and not in the sun, because no ray of sunshine finds its way through the thick foliage above us.

Another hut. Two men lying on the slope outside: one has a brown cap over his face; the other holds a bottle of spirits. The one with the bottle waves and laughs when he catches sight of us. Then takes a drink and leans back again. A few yards away from them a woman sits against a tree with a child in her lap.

The silence under the trees is broken by a strange dull sound.

A young woman is grinding maize in an old-fashioned mortar. She wears a ragged pale blue blouse which covers one breast only. A small bunch of runny-nosed, half-naked children stands around her with big inquiring eyes. The woman sends the biggest one away through the trees. When he comes back he is carrying two low wooden stools.

'I should like to have offered you some tea,' Mary Musangi tells me the young woman says.

I ask if she belongs to the women's group.

She doesn't. She can't afford it. She has three children of her own and also has the care of her dead sister's children. Her sister never had a husband and so there are no co-wives to take on the responsibility. She is responsible for three of her own and her sister's three children, the young woman with the mortar, and her husband is out of work. He just lies in the hut and sleeps. . . .

I have a packet of sweets in my bag, orange sweets I bought at Heathrow. I give them to the children. The aunt-mother smiles; Mary Musangi gives me a scornful look and chews her gum.

We've come out of the dark wood into the sun. There are fields on both sides of the path. The next house we come to is like the first; built of crumbling rotten planks by long-departed whites. An elderly woman is in the yard washing up. Small children, some clothed, some not. Cackling hens. A few goats that walk around untethered. A young woman with a screaming child on her back comes back from the field with coconuts in one hand and a long knife in the other.

Little stools round a table. Coconut milk. A dream of a bakery. Fresh bread to sell for money. Money for food, for clothes, money for schooling . . . Both these women

59

belong to the women's group, they are mother-in-law and daughter-in-law; one looks after the other's children, the other works in the field for both of them. They have a common dream of an oven.

'We'd be glad to have it here in our yard, we have said so to the group.'

Over the coconuts, the children's faces, the piled up washing-up, the chickens and goats, wafts a scent of new-baked bread.

We take another route back to the main road. A long stretch without any soothing green crowns above us, a dry winding cart track with sun-dried, grey-green fields on both sides, later low brushwood, taller bushes, then level ground again.

Now I am in front. Mary Musangi walks behind me; she struggles on her high heels, groans in the heat. I put my bag on my head for a sun-hat. I think of the African women's long walk to fetch water and wonder how far I'd manage to walk like that without falling.

At last we have black asphalt in front of us. It's only a few hundred yards to where the Tototo Centre's car is parked. I start to stride out but suddenly feel I'm alone. When I turn round I see Mary Musangi standing at the side of the straight level road pulling off her brandy-coloured tights and yellow shoes.

Back in town we stop at a restaurant on one of the main streets. Campari on the rocks. Lemon slices. The driver drinks ice-cold cola. The chairs we sit in are white plastic. A few tables away from us a man in his twenties sits giving a European woman an African-look hairstyle. Ranged along the roadside, worn-out cabs wait for fares.

My interpreter is no longer my interpreter and she

wears a kind, good-natured smile. She's thrown away her chewing-gun. She refuses a cigarette with thanks.

Around us are men and women in suits and dresses, well-dressed people; at the neighbouring tables, walking along the street.

We've been sitting here all morning; Mary Musangi and I. The dream about fresh loaves is something we've read about; the old settlers' houses, the huts in the shadowy forest, the fierce sunlight over the dry path all belong to tableaux, sets from some strange theatre or other.

'Are you hungry, Mary?' I ask.

The other nods.

Under the table lie her shoes, yellow and scuffed, beside her naked feet.

The blind woman of Kakamega

A blind woman in Kakamega walks round and round her little hut. She's humpbacked, but she holds her head high and her blind milky-white eyes look ahead; past the trees behind the tiny patch of ground towards Lake Victoria, Mount Elgon, Turkana or the coast, east of the sun and west of the moon, depending on where she is in her circling of the hut.

The first time I heard about her was in a Steak House in Nairobi on the second floor of a grey brick building on Kenyatta Avenue; steak and red wine with a Norwegian woman member of the Peace Corps.

'People seem to change a lot when they've been here a while,' says Grete. 'Before we came down here we were set on doing something to help, worrying over history, why it is that the world is divided into rich and poor, we wanted to come to Africa to give a hand in putting things to rights, a scrap of help if nothing more. . . .'

'But then?'

'It's not as easy as that. We were never well off at home, it was a big family, but I've had a little pad of my own the last few years. And then I came here to be a teacher in Kakamega and was assigned a whole little house to myself. A whole house, maybe nothing to brag about compared to Norway but where Kenya is concerned, when I know what sort of homes the kids I teach have to put up with. . . . And that's not all; I inherited a house help from the bloke who'd been here before me, as if I'd ever dreamed of having help. I came here to offer what skills I have, not to be waited on.'

'Couldn't you give her notice, then?'

'It's a man. And he has a wife and a flock of kids. If I give him notice it means a whole family with no income. Children without money for school. A family without food. . . .'

Grete from the youth club in Sagene wonders what the club members would say if they saw her as she sits and marks exercise books in her sitting room in Kakamega while a man in his forties washes the floor around her feet, washes her clothes in the yard outside the house, irons them in the kitchen, puts them neatly away in her drawers. . . .

This isn't the way we usually talk when we meet. When Peace Corps members get together they tend to go on about who has done better than the others. Why someone has the right to a free car and not others. Or we chat about demanding Africans who think they can have whatever they ask for from foreign aid organizations. . . .

Grete in Kakamega, with a tail of children behind her when she's out for an afternoon jog, a tail of inquisitive laughing children.

'There's so much that's sad,' she says.

Then tells me about the blind woman, walking and walking round her lopsided little hut.

'When she works on her plot, she crawls.'

An old woman who sows and weeds and harvests a crop she cannot see. Who drags herself along on all fours, with feet and knees and rough worn palms chafing against dry twigs and straw.

'Amazing how she manages. Amazing the snakes don't bite her. . . .'

The second time I heard about her was at the Peace Corps Centre in Kisumu.

I had retreated into a corner of the sofa; partly to look

through my notes, partly because the others were engaged in a noisy discussion of internal Norad affairs. We had been out for dinner at an Indian restaurant; meat and rice and leaf-thin pepper bread. An elegant eating place in Kenya's 'Little Bombay': velvet and mirrors and shiny black tables, gold and silken saris at neighbouring tables. Wine with the food, more wine when we came back to the Peace Corps Centre.

I've brought my glass and cigarettes over to the sofa, while the others still sit round the heavy wooden table in the middle of the room; five youngsters discussing a problem with the new local Norad co-ordinator. It is about a basket factory in Turkana. Two Norwegian girls have created job opportunities for 150 people, the only sizeable labour market in this dry inhospitable district; 150 people who sit in the shade weaving baskets. Now they need another employee; someone to take on the marketing of the produce in the capital. But so far the Norad administration has been unwilling to grant further funding.

'But we have to see it through,' says an excited young man.

'Are you sure this idea isn't just as spontaneous as the fishing project?' asks the co-ordinator.

The fish from Lake Turkana. Norwegian grant aid for fishing equipment, refrigerated vehicle; fish driven the long, long way from Turkana to Nairobi, where only wealthy ambassadors' wives could afford to buy it.

'But this is different. . . .'

'Aren't these baskets exactly the same as the ones you can buy in the market? From men and women who sit outside the houses and weave them. And sell them for much less than the Turkana baskets?' the co-ordinator asks.

'But we really must follow up what we've started on. . . .'

'Sometimes you people in offices don't seem to see a hand in front of your faces. . . .'

'Blind as the woman in Kakamega. . . .'

As the woman in Kakamega? I raise my eyes and look at them. They hold back. Didn't come to Kisumu to pick a quarrel. But it's the wine. The urge to get on with things.

'You're not here as a journalist too?' they ask me.

'No. I shan't publish your disagreements in Norway. Anyway, I wasn't listening. I was thinking about my. . .'

The blind woman in Kakamega.

'What about her?' I ask Torodd, the teacher who mentioned her.

'I was in Kakamega before I came to Bondo. She had the responsibility of a grandchild, a girl who left school during the year I was there, one of the best pupils. Just before the exam I was asked to select a girl for further education at the agricultural school in Kiambu; they could take only one from each village, and we had to choose a girl who was intelligent but poor, so poor that she would otherwise have no chance of further schooling. I chose her, the blind woman's grandchild. . . .'

A few days later I arrived in Kiambu.

I sit on the terrace in front of the principal's house, in a deep basket chair opposite the sunbronzed Norwegian head teacher, and drink cold beer in the cool leafy shade. He tells me about the school which is an example of how foreign aid workers themselves correct the mistakes they make as they discover them; for years they tried to teach men to bore for wells and construct waterworks until they realized it was the women they had to start with, it was the women's responsibility to get water. Just as it was the women who shouldered most of the responsibility for the farming.

This was the reason for the agricultural school for girls in Kiambu. Twenty-eight pupils aged between fourteen and seventeen, from various different districts, tribes and religions. A pilot scheme. The pupils stay for two years. Then they go back to their villages to share their newfound knowledge with relatives and neighbours. The agricultural school in Kiambu will diffuse knowledge the country over. It will speed progress and modernization.

The two pupils who show me round are Lilian and Ebby, one from the Luo tribe and the other a Somali, one small and light-footed, the other long-legged and awkward.

Ebby and Lilian walk on the path in front of me in dark blue working trews and green sneakers. Through the lovely garden, through the enclosure with the newborn calves, Christmas and Happy New Year, who lick our fingers, into the little house with the red-painted milking machine, past the field and down to the artificial dam that supplies the school with water. Lovely slant-eyed Lilian who talks all the time, explains the ingenious piping system which makes the water run up the hill to the pumps by the field, to the garden with the rabbit hutches, into the houses, the kitchen and lavatories. Proper water-closets which she demonstrates when we return.

Lilian and Ebby who show me the classrooms, the books, the wall charts, who invite me to lunch in the pupils' canteen, to cabbage soup and white bread, and afterwards ask me if I'd like to see the room they share.

A tiny room with bunk beds, writing desk, chair and two cupboards. Colourful postcards on the cupboard doors. Pale yellow curtains at the window. I ask them if they look forward to going home again after their studies

69

are ended. Ebby's face lights up; she's excited, she is engaged, her sweetheart is proud of her being at agricultural school. But Lilian doesn't reply. She sits on the bottom bunk, strokes the soft blanket. The first bed of her own, I think, her own bedclothes, blanket, the first cupboard of her own. . . .

'I'm not going to get married,' she says.

'Why not?'

'No.'

Ebby stretches her long neck, she pulls the curtain aside, looks out at the other pupils sitting in groups out there where they're sewing or playing hairdressers with each other. Her friend's sudden seriousness embarrasses her. Embarrasses her by bringing the mean little huts they've come from out of the shadows into this light and cosy room.

Sitting on the bed there I hear the story of a young widow. Of Lilian's father who died when Lilian was quite small and her mother who married again and vanished.

'Why couldn't you stay with her and her new husband?'

'He didn't want to know about me.'

'But surely she came to see you.'

'Never.'

'Why not?'

'He probably wouldn't let her.'

'But who looked after you then?'

'My grandmother.'

The blind woman in Kakamega.

When Lilian's two years are over she'll have to go back to the village she came from. In her brown cardboard suitcase there'll be papers testifying that her head is full of knowledge about drainage, livestock, nutrition and agriculture. Perhaps there will be a small plaque on the wall of the dining hall in Kiambu announcing she was the best pupil in her class.

Back to Kakamega with knowledge from Kiambu to pass on and spread over the country to create progress and prosperity. Back to a little hut with threadbare bedclothes and chipped pots and a scrap of land, to grandmother who walks round and round her little hut. Round and round. Humpbacked but still with her head held high and her milky-white eyes looking ahead; over the trees behind the shamba towards Lake Victoria, Mount Elgon, Turkana or the coast, east of the sun and west of the moon, depending on where she is in her wanderings.

High walls covered with green ivy

Behind a high wall covered with green ivy lies Rita. In a big garden behind wrought-iron gates, beside an S-shaped swimming pool, on a flat sunbed upholstered in water-resistant material patterned with fiery yellow flowers, one hand hanging loosely down from the edge of the sunbed so her fingertips almost reach the ground, Rita Johansen from Stovner and Norway lies feeling bored. She is naked. Her body is brown and glistening. The faintest of lines shows the design of her bikini, under a towel beside her in case someone should suddenly arrive. On the other side of the sunbed on the stylish pink marble that surrounds the S of the pool like a curving belt, is a golden morning drink. And beside the drink: an ashtray, a lighter and a packet of Petteroe's Mild rolling tobacco.

Rita Johansen is smoking. She sips her drink. She lies with eyes closed breathing in the smell of the fiery yellow flowered cover, counting smells to keep her thoughts at a distance. Almost without realizing it she reels them off: the smell of her suncream, sunburned skin (the smell of pigment?), the smell of the fiery yellow flowered material, a mixture of plastic and cloth which also smells of sweat, suncream, sunburned skin (pigment?) and chlorinated water. The smell of smoke. Of grass. The smell of the deodorant she uses and of Chloé. Deodorant under her arms and a little drop of Chloé on her neck. A good and an unsophisticated perfume that blend to form Rita's Smell. Someone has told her that a couple of times; tried to teach her not to mix perfumes like this, tried to teach her not to ruin Chloé, to use that only and not use perfumed deodorants. But there are some things Rita from Stovner and Oslo has never bothered to make use of; such as hints on how to be a real lady.

Her mind meanders. At times conscious of the smells, at others not. Hits on: will the doctor she'll be talking to this morning keep quiet about what he'll learn? And images come: the pale pink palms of Gabriel N's hands. His eyes; round with wonder. Rita shivers as if struck by chill under the hot sun.

She reaches for her drink. Rolls a fresh cigarette. She hears a telephone ring in the distance. A long minute passes, then Ainike comes out to the veranda and calls in her gentle and ever-cheerful voice: 'Mrs Johansen, someone wants to talk to you. . . .'

'Yes, that's right, he'll be coming. . . .'
'So your husband suggested we might drop in, if that's not troubling you?'
'Yes, yes, of course. . . .'

She replaces the receiver. Straightens her back and sees to her surprise that the woman in the mirror behind the telephone table is standing there without a stitch. Didn't she put something on? She usually does. For Ainike's sake if nothing else.

She stays there and studies her own body. Thighs, stomach, she's put on some weight; she eats too much, drinks too much. Breasts: flexible breasts, firm and round, Rita is proud of her breasts. Shoulders: slightly angular. Face: the broad nose is there as usual, and the lips that Jan Arne calls greedy. He used to hold her a little way from him, gaze into her face, take it in little by little, his narrow blue eyes glinting with lust: greedy lips, he'd say, with respect. Perhaps he still says it. Perhaps he still gazes into her face on the rare occasions when they come together as woman and man, she can't remember. Can't remember.

In the shower Rita wonders what she should have said to have put off the young Peace Corps teacher who just rang. She's met him before, several times. A moody, reserved, fair young man. Now his sister has come to visit him. She has been travelling around and has probably picked up malaria. That was why he had phoned Jan Arne at the embassy, to ask about a doctor. That was why Jan Arne had told him to ring Rita, because he knew she was expecting Dr Fredrik Hansteen to call some time during the morning. For some small complaint and a drink, Jan Arne thinks. But he's wrong. Rita needs help for an abortion. Rita is pregnant. Not by Jan Arne but by a black waiter called Gabriel N. from the Bellevue Hotel. That's what the label on his black and green livery says: Gabriel N.

That's what Rita wants to talk to Fredrik Hansteen about alone.

She's sitting by the little table on the marble terrace around the pool when the guests arrive. She hears the sound of their car stopping in front of the wrought-iron gates, pictures the teacher opening them, driving in, stopping again and parking in front of the house. Or is it Fredrik? She sits with her back to the house looking at the water; she wears white knee-length trousers and a white shirt with Fly in black letters on the chest. Fly.

'It's probably only a touch of food poisoning,' says the student sister.

'It's quite definitely malaria,' her brother, the Peace Corps teacher, says gently but firmly.

Ainike has made them tea; boiled the water, poured it on the tea leaves, brought out the tray with pot and cups, sugar bowl and milk jug. Rita has thanked her with a smile, put on her sunglasses and fetched herself a fresh drink.

'What are the symptoms?' she asks.

'It started yesterday evening. High temperature. I was shaking and freezing in the heat, put on all the clothes I had, long skirts on top of long trousers . . . vomiting. Diarrhoea. Pains all over. Typical flu symptoms.'

'Typical malaria,' says her brother.

'But now I'm all right again?'

'Typical malaria,' says Rita. 'You get an attack each time the eggs in the blood hatch out, which is once a day, at the same time. A few hours later you can be as right as rain, and then it hits you again after twenty-four hours.'

'Just what I told you,' her brother says.

'It's not dangerous provided you take the antidote. Don't you have any of it?'

'I left it at Tomas's school. We have to go back there. . . .'

'Fredrik will let you have some. You just relax here till he comes. Have a dip if you'd like to. . . .'

Three people on sunbeds at the edge of a pool. Rita has taken off her clothes again; apart from her brief black bikini pants and sunglasses she lies naked on her back under the sun. Tomas, the Peace Corps teacher, sits and dries his face after a dip. Ainike has just brought him some beer. Juice for his sister. What more could they want?

Rita thinks of Gabriel N. She thinks about thinking of him, glances at her guests through her dark glasses and thinks she baffles them. She's different. Full of secrets. She wishes the two of them in hell. Or herself.

*

Far back in the land of remembrance there's another black man. He was an American, he may have studied in Oslo for a while, Rita doesn't know. But she once heard him give a lecture, some time just after the mid-sixties at the 7 Club. Twenty or thirty women on chairs facing a black man who stood leaning up against a wall. On the second floor. A tough athletic man who poured shame and guilt over the pale female faces in front of him. In an incisive and at the same time monotonous deep masculine voice he cast a spell over the assembly, over-powered the assembly, bound them to their chairs, to their pillories, to the grim historical conscience of the white race.

Rita was one of the youngest in the hall and it was quite by chance that she was there at all. Half-way through she tore herself away and went down to buy a bottle of wine. With wine, glass and tobacco she went back again and stood by herself at the back of the room by the stove. And she knew the performance being enacted was a performance. It was nothing to do with the guilt or responsibility of the white race; it was about how a black American prepared his nightly meal, how he manipulated twenty or thirty white women till they just lay there gasping and crying, 'Yes! Yes!'

Rita had sat down at a table there at the back, drunk her wine and smoked and followed the lecturer with narrowed eyes. When he had finished, his dizzy audience staggered downstairs to the bar and she sat on alone. With three rows of empty chairs between her and a black American. He came over to her and sat down at her table. Without asking he drank from her glass, rolled her tobacco, she used Egbert's then.

She's slept with two black men in her life. With an interval of almost twenty years.

*

To think it was twenty years since she began to understand. More than twenty years since the first long
marches against the atom bomb; she was very young then
but she took part. The fight for disarmament. Peace
work. Study groups and seminars on Why war? Why
hunger? History. Economics.

Blindern University, Oslo, autumn 1968. Preparatory.
The basic course in political science next spring. Then on
to history, perhaps sociology.

In the lift at the sv block she came across Jan Arne; she
has a strong feeling they slept together, or rather stood,
that time in the lift, and it was then she started Kurt.

'Did he say when he would come?'

The sick student's voice is thin and faint.

'No,' Rita says curtly.

As if she was responsible for this girl? Fredrik isn't
coming to see her, but Rita. Then she makes an effort to
sound kinder: 'Why don't you have a swim too?'

'D'you think that's a good thing?' the other asks.

'It won't make any difference to the malaria. If you'd
like to, that is.'

The brother and sister bathe. Rita looks at them through
her sunglasses and smokes. Ainike makes lunch for
them, comes out with trays of plates and glasses and good
food; she puts a cloth on the garden table, lays it, smiles,
goes back into the house with straight back and head held
high. She's doing a job. Rita says it to herself, inside her
head. Ainike does a job. Like any other job. She comes at
the appointed time, does her job and leaves again. She
gets wages. Ainike gets as her pay some of the money Jan
Arne earns at the embassy. The brother and sister praise
the food, directing their words at Rita. She wonders if
they're making fun of her.

She hopes Fredrik will come soon so the girl can get her Fanzidars and go.

'Have you been to a lot of places?' she asks.

The student takes this as an encouragement to launch out. She describes her trips: Johannesburg, Harare, a car tour to Matabeleland. By air to Nairobi. By train through Kenya, to and fro, a boat on Lake Victoria . . . she has been travelling for nearly two months with money she's been saving up for several years; the journey ends here with her brother.

'What d'you think of it then?'

More encouragement.

She thinks a lot. She no longer seems ill; Inger-Johanne, music student from Blindern and Ila, is bright and concentrated as she leans across the table towards Rita and fills the air between and around them with words.

Polygamy. Childbirth. Hunger. Childbirth. Polygamy.

Her voice is indignant, almost agitated. Rita looks at the denim jacket Inger-Johanne has dropped on the lawn and thinks she hates denim.

Men who decide everything. Women forced to creep in on all fours to serve the chap's tea. Who are not allowed to talk to their husband before he gives them leave. Men who sleep with all and sundry. Who do what the hell they like. Little mud huts with swarms of dirty children.

'They don't even know about chimneys here,' says Inger-Johanne. 'They cook on a fire right at the back of the hut in the furthest corner and sit there with streaming red eyes in all the smoke. Stupid creatures.'

Ainike comes out to clear the table, and she asks if they'd like coffee.

'But why should our Western culture have to be the

best sort?' says Rita. 'If people want to live in round mud huts that's their affair. They can put up a mud hut in a day. At least then the children get closeness and warmth; better that than lonely little girls and boys in their own rooms in blocks of flats in Stovner. . . .'

'Yes, but . . .'

'Why can't white people stop meddling all the time. Why can't we ever leave the Africans in peace. We come out here and pull our own family programme down over their ears, on with sterilization, on with free condoms. . . .'

She's interrupted by a shout from the veranda. It's not the doctor, it's Kurt. Sixteen years old, pupil at the international school, son of Rita and Jan Arne. Kurt comes across the grass towards them, shining-eyed and sweaty under his fair mop of hair, wearing high boots and riding breeches and a thin T-shirt. He shakes hands with the guests. Rita gets up, walks barefoot over the soft grass, up the steps into the living room to pour herself a brandy to go with the coffee. She stands there on the fleecy carpet and looks out of the window at the garden. Slim broad-shouldered Kurt. Easy and lively with those two he's never seen before. Polite and reassuring. Rita takes a big gulp of the brown liquid. A wave of nausea streams through her. She presses her hands against the shiny mahogany, swallows, shuts her eyes, gathers all her will to combat her unruly stomach. It's her pituitary gland, neither malaria nor food poisoning. The result of her adventure with Gabriel N. She straightens her back and blinks. Forces down another mouthful.

Sometimes she's walked through slum quarters and imagined that now she's been robbed. Now. By that man approaching her. Or by that one. Or in the market-place. Every time she gets out her purse to buy something or other she visualizes the fingers; long black fingers snatching at her money. But it never happens. Or at least it hasn't yet. It doesn't happen because she is not afraid. She knows her own hatred is stronger than theirs. For the time being. Because hatred requires knowledge, knowledge that she has and they lack. She despises them for not hating.

Gabriel N., who in his own free country was unable to see himself her equal, who didn't dare touch her in new places until she asked him to. His soft, firm hands she had to guide around her body. Big strong Gabriel N. like a little little boy in her arms, even when he knew it was allowed he could hardly let himself believe it; permission might be withdrawn at any moment. As it was. Gabriel N. He probably never wanted her in the first place.

'Do you think he will be here soon?' mumbles the Peace Corps teacher.

Brother and sister sit idly with their feet in the water. They do not smoke or drink. Rita flicks her ash into the air and is half-way through her second brandy.

'Maybe he won't be coming at all,' she says, 'you never know with doctors.'

She rises abruptly, pulls off her sunglasses and dives into the pool. Rita, with open eyes and hands straight in front of her, like a sputnik flying towards the bottom at an angle. She holds her breath, but she could let go. She could draw breath, fill her lungs with this transparent, wet . . . she reaches the surface again. Comes up, shakes the water out of her eyes, lies on her back, floating, floating. . . .

Brother and sister whisper together. Are they about to go? The sooner the better. She lies with closed eyes like a plant, a water-lily, she's thought that herself, a long narrow plant in an S-shaped pool in the centre of a lawn surrounded by high walls. Like Sleeping Beauty. But she's awake. She's been awake the whole time.

They talk about the weather. The latest news. What's happening in Norway. Safe subjects chosen with care by the music student and her brother as if they are afraid Rita will flare up. They get on her nerves.

Kurt phones to say he's staying with a friend. Jan Arne phones to say he has an unexpected meeting.

They have a late dinner on the veranda, prepared by Rita herself; Ainike has finished work and gone. Rita cooks well. If she hadn't been going to be an historian and political scientist she might have been a chef. But she became neither.

When at last Fredrik Hansteen drives up the avenue towards the black wrought-iron gates it's almost dark. When no one answers his ring he finds his own way through the house. Rita is on the veranda. In a long skirt and little sweater, Rita, barefoot, leans against one of the two pillars that hold up the sun roof. Rita hears his steps behind her; feels him stop only a yard away from her, stop without saying anything. Rita thinks Fredrik Hansteen will stand there looking at her for a long time; at her back, her long hair, and it strikes her she can kill a lot of time letting herself be seduced by Norwegians in Africa.

She offers him a drink.

They sit outside. Their faces are soft in the light of the candles on the table. The young doctor is tired. He was delayed this morning, has had a long day behind the wheel. He forgets to ask what Rita wanted to see him about. Suddenly he knows only that there was no reason at all, no reason other than that lying like a dark secret in her eyes, in the way she tosses her hair. She sits with her legs crossed, her face turned in half-profile towards him. In her hand a half-smoked Camel. No more roll-ups.

'It's so lonely out there where I live,' says Fredrik Hansteen.

A pale violet moon shines through the trees. The sound of car brakes comes from far away. Rita goes inside to put on some music. She hears steps and voices overhead. She has thoroughly subdued the brother and sister; Inger-Johanne is up there in the guest room; twenty-four hours have passed, a new batch of eggs has hatched, she's lying there with a fever, paroxysms of cold and attacks of heat, vomiting and diarrhoea.

Rita puts on Stan Getz and Johnny Smith. Moonlight in Vermont for Fredrik Hansteen.

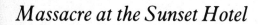

Massacre at the Sunset Hotel

When I went down the steps to the pool at the Sunset Hotel only two people were there before me. One was in the water; a big fat man who snorted like a hippo as he shovelled himself to and fro, to and fro through the green water. He was white. The other was black; with a long narrow face and sharp features. He wore a black suit and shirt, black shoes and socks; the eyes that fell on me as I sat down at the table next to him were black and expressionless. He made me think 'American'.

I ordered beer and a sandwich, slipped off my shoes, put my feet on a chair and leafed through a newspaper while I waited.

The red-faced swimmer left the water and sat himself down fat and dripping wet at the same table as the black man. I thought 'Irishman'. His face wore a mildly transfigured and slightly childish expression. I thought 'Missionary'.

The missionary addressed me: asked where I was from and what I was doing in Kisumu. He told me he loved Africa and the Africans and would probably never go back to Ireland.

My food and beer arrived.

More guests arrived while I ate; a mother and father and four little pink and peeling children. All six changed into swimsuits and the grown-ups launched into swimming lessons at the shallow end of the pool. I gathered from their voices that the number of missionaries had risen to seven. I turned my head and met the eyes of the man in black who was stroking his armpit outside his jacket. He made no response to my smile.

After giving my lunch time to settle I went down to the ladies' cloakroom to change. The white walls were covered with tiny pale brown ants and one of the lavatories was leaking. When I went back to the pool the Irish missionary was in the water again, and the big family sat under a garden umbrella eating the picnic they'd brought with them. I pulled in my stomach and dived. The Irishman smiled foolishly and clapped. He played at being a sea-monster; swam under water, under me, shot up again with the same silly smile.

'Do you love Africa?'

'Sure.'

He swam unpleasantly close and whispered in my ear:

'Masai.'

Masai. The man in black with the Colt was a Masai. I shot a glance at him. He followed us with his eyes while he paid the waiter for a beer.

Not an American, a Masai. Stubbornly isolated nomad. Firm grasp of customs and traditions. Songs and dances. Rituals. About the only remaining market for glass beads. Minute beads in various colours, put together in special patterns with a special symbolic significance. Belts that indicate if a woman is married. Head-dresses indicating she is still fertile. Necklaces. Ear-rings. Glass beads were originally brought to Kenya by Arabian slaves and ivory traders. Later they were imported by merchants on the coast, at one time from Italy, now chiefly from Czechoslovakia.

The tough poor Masai who live as they have done for centuries. With their cattle. With their simple life style. With their illiteracy and their pride.

*

I came out of the water with the Irish missionary in my wake. On my way past the bar I asked for another beer. While I dried myself on my big yellow towel more people came down the steps.

Two young black women. One in silver-coloured trews, the other in a red dress with one shoulder strap. High-heeled shoes. The one in the dress went and changed into a bikini, the other stayed as she was, with a whisky.

Shortly afterwards two Asians arrived, in business suits, each with his little metal brief-case full of microprocessors, diamonds, dollars or other important papers.

The two men sat together. The two women together. Then a sudden change. A man and a woman at each table. And in the next scene they disappeared, first one couple and then the other, while the women's belongings were left by their original table; a pair of sunglasses, a chiffon scarf and the red dress over the back of a chair.

The black-sleeved arm of the Masai on my left twitched slightly. With narrowed gaze he watched the Asians and the two women go off.

A twittering came from little red birds and larger black ones in the trees beyond the pool. Behind the trees was Lake Victoria, calm and pale blue. I knew that a big passenger boat waited in Kisumu harbour; it would sail as soon as the frontier with Tanzania was reopened, any time now.

'Strange there can be drought in a country with such a huge lake,' said the missionary as if following my gaze past the birds down towards the shining blue.

He talked about the firm that was to lay water pipes, a complete network of irrigation that would make large areas of the surrounding districts far more productive than they were today. The plans were made years ago.

Money poured in from one organization after the other but nothing happened because the managers of the firm stuffed all the money into their own pockets and vanished, followed by new managers who stayed for a while until they too vanished.

The Masai snapped his fingers for another beer.

The Irishman sweated in the sun. I lit another cigarette and started to write home; postcards with jungle jokes on them.

I heard a big splash followed a few seconds later by a sharp crack. I shut my eyes. Wasn't this what I'd been waiting for all the time? One missionary less, I thought, recalling the Masai's dark expressionless gaze and his hand on the Colt under his arm. I stayed there with closed eyes, not sure I wanted to look; the gaping visitors on the other side of the pool, the water slowly turning from transparent green to cloudy red. . . .

Light steps behind me made me open my eyes despite myself. It was the waiter with a dustpan and brush. The Masai had dropped his glass on the paving stones. Beer and glass fragments were strewn around. The missionary climbed out of the water again, picked up his towel and went off to change. One of the two women, the one in silver trews, came down the steps again. She ordered a drink. I took note of her pony tail as she went back to her table, made up of thin black plaits interwoven with drops of silver.

Not until the Irishman and the Masai were leaving did I see that the African was handicapped; one leg was deformed and his right shoulder made little jerks as he slowly dragged himself up the steps that led to the car park.

The waiter was still clearing up the broken pieces of his glass.

Men's pride

Sonia sweats under the white sheet. The air in the room is stagnant; it smells sour and it smells of hospital. There are five of them in here, and none of the others has given birth yet either. Five silent women, waiting.

Sonia strokes her stomach, thinks she feels a soft little response; no kicking, but still; a movement, a reaction. Had it been like this the other times?

Joel walks along the narrow path that crosses the patch belonging to the school. Withered harvested maize stalks. Sprouting potatoes. Banana palms with green unripe bunches under the leaves. The sky above him is grey-blue with mist. It's rained, and the earth is damp and black, steaming. Big, gleaming blue flies swarm around him, around the plants. Joel gets to the end of the field, crosses the green turf and makes for the school buildings. His face looks hard. Closed.

He gives a maths lesson to a class of boys. In a detached manner he reels off figures, formulae, writes problems on the blackboard which they work at, necks bent, at their desks. Joel sits behind the desk with shoulders hunched. His body feels uncomfortable; slowly he realizes he needs to urinate.

Joel, Sonia thinks. She's trembling under the clammy sheet. She wrinkles her forehead; tries to think good thoughts.

She recalls her last year in school, the love letters from

Joel, the thrill every time she opened one, the weight of it in her hands. And then the time when the headmaster confiscated a whole week's love letters to the girls; many of them in the top class had fiancés or boy friends who lived in other places. It was to teach them a lesson, he told them after a whole week had gone by. He told them he'd opened their letters, read them, and was now going to burn them. In front of their eyes he had held out first one letter, then another, read out the name it was addressed to, put a match to it and swung it to and fro in the air like a little torch until he almost burned his fingers. Then he had let go of it, looked at them with a mixture of severity and malice and ground out the last of the flames with the heel of his shoe.

Sonia remembers her own disbelief. Some of the girls had been on the verge of tears. Others stood with heads bowed to hide the anger they felt at this man who stood there pulling envelopes one by one from his pockets; slowly and almost smilingly, waiting as long as possible before reading the names, raising the tension among the girls higher, higher. . . .

The next day they got up before daylight. Without a sound they crept out of the school, marched through dark and dawning the five miles to the nearest village and police station, charged the headmaster with theft and marched the five miles back in the morning sunshine, proud, elated, laughing along the dusty highway.

Sonia will never forget it. She can't imagine what made them dare that impossible campaign that took them from one authority to another; the malicious headmaster and astonished chief constable; he couldn't believe his eyes, as he'd sat behind his desk and gaped at them when they crowded into his little office.

'But . . . but why? Why did he do that?' the policeman stammered at last.

'He says reading love letters makes us neglect our school work. . . .'

'I see. Of course. And I suppose you write replies to the letters you get?'

Did the policeman think it was reasonable to steal people's letters then?

He hadn't answered that. But when the girls got back to school they found the head prepared and the main gate and doors to all the buildings locked. The caretaker had been told not to let them in; they were expelled, he'd have no more of them. And with wild yells and a courage Sonia hadn't known they owned, the girls had climbed the fence and torn off in the direction of the head's house. Woe to him who takes other people's letters. Woe to him who steals and reads and burns others' personal, private, wonderful, burning love letters.

She smiles to herself in the narrow hospital bed. Smiles and thinks of the letters from Joel, which may not have been especially burning and exciting, but were hers. From him. Then her smile fades, and her mind concentrates on her big stomach again. Is there life there? Any little kick? Pains?

Joel takes his lunch break with the other teachers. They sit under the trees outside the administration block, eat and drink tea and milk. Pupils come out of the dining hall on the other side of the wide stretch of lawn in ones and twos; some of them start tossing a ball over a net, and a flock of pink and white birds take off in fright, at the same second, as if with a single will they fly up and disappear behind the trees.

'How is Sonia getting on?' asks the English teacher, a white woman.

'She's in hospital.'

'Have you phoned in?'

Joel shakes his head. He hasn't phoned. He doesn't intend to phone either. He went to the matatu with her yesterday evening, supported her while they stood waiting in the ditch, he gave her money for the ride home, and watched until the little bus had gone right out of sight.

English Maggie looks over her glasses at him. He looks back. At the sharp blue eyes, the iron-grey hair, at her thin lips. She can ask away as long as she likes, she won't get any answer out of him.

Sonia is in labour, that's her affair. When she comes back it will be Joel's. But never Maggie's.

Joel who wanted to have her before she'd taken her exam. Sonia lies on her back and looks up at the grey-white ceiling. When she can manage to think of just that she smiles. Joel's strong hands, his lithe sensual body that wanted her, Sonia, and her alone.

But he had had to wait. She wanted to finish her schooling first. And then she didn't finish it after all. Because of his love letters. And the others'.

Then he did get her. Like a pact sealed with happy smiles.

The wedding. One thousand shillings Joel had paid for her. One thousand shillings he had earned by small jobs of work outside his study time. She remembered her father's words about having respect for him.

'A sensible woman learns from her husband's words. A sensible woman learns how to obey.'

Sonia looks at the ceiling. She pulls the sheet over her head and hides herself. There's no other world than this soft, dusky sheet-world. There's no universe except herself, herself and the big stomach. An anchor, a weight attaching her to the strange bed; why couldn't she have stayed at home for the birth like she had the other times? It was Joel who wanted her to come into hospital. And she had complied. Joel had wanted it, wanted her to be in the doctors' hands, under clammy white sheets. She feels dampness; on her diaphragm, her throat and neck, her hands run with sweat, her mouth is dry, why is nothing happening? Why can't the baby kick, kick hard at her guts and her ribs, like it had the last few months, why don't the pains get going again as they did hours ago. . . .

Joel has finished for the day. He packs his case and feels eyes on the back of his head. Maggie. Maggie, who thinks there should be a special text book for East Africans because they never learn to speak English properly anyway. Maggie, who apes the kids and says 'How is you today?' and laughs. Weren't the English supposed to get out in 1964? But some of us had to stay and show a little responsibility, Maggie had said once.

'Have you phoned to ask how she is now?' asks the grey-haired woman.

'No.'

'Why not?'

'No.'

They stand there facing each other. Maggie shuts the outside door with her body.

'You can come to supper with me if you like,' she says.

'Thank you,' Joel mumbles. 'Thank you, but . . . '

He comes to a stop. Looks down at the floor.

'Perhaps you'd rather eat with your mother?'

Joel nods. He feels sweat running down inside his shirt. He practically forces himself past her and out, into the afternoon sun, the blue sky, out on to the grass that's softer and greener after the rain last night. He strides off, crosses the yard and goes out on the road. What right has

Maggie to rule over him? What right have foreign women to meddle in his relationship with his wife? If women haven't got what it takes, what's the use of throwing money away on visits to the doctor time and again. . . ? With a furious kick, he sends a stone hurtling across the road. Hasn't he sent her to the hospital, anyway?

Joel lies on his back on the bed in the hut. He thinks of Sonia. Her fine, firm back, light steps and eyes that are different from the rest, shy and frightened like an animal's. They weren't like that before. When she was still at school. Before the first pregnancy. . . . Bloody women, Joel gets up, roughly pours some water in the wash bowl, washes the upper part of himself and changes his shirt. Full of restlessness, he rushes out again and across the road.

Joel is in a bar. On a tall rickety stool with one arm resting on the counter, the other hand holding a glass. His eyes shine feverishly but his hands are steady and his voice clear when he speaks.

Five or six men sit side by side. Most have shabby trousers, some wear hats to shade their eyes from the low evening sun. They exchange a few words now and then. Look at the wall of the long narrow kiosk that calls itself a bar, look out, at the road, the scrub behind it, the sinking ball of sun.

Joel empties his glass, slides down from the stool and leaves. He straightens his back, feels his body strong and supple, Joel's firm legs striding out almost at a run are Joel's, the broad shoulders, Joel is a grown man in his own country, has studied at the unversity in Nairobi, he's a teacher earning money, Joel is Joel is Joel is a man. . . .

*

Strange faces lift up the mattress she lies on and carry her into another room. Sonia clutches the sheet; she has strong pains and her eyes are closed. The pains are a relief, not bad, only good, good because that's how it *should* be, how it is. And it's different this time, she can feel it is, the pains are stronger, more regular, surely? But she's frightened all the same, gripped by a sharp, white shining fear behind the closed eyes. She holds her breath in fright, grips her stomach hard with sharp fingers, hunting for living limbs. . . .

She feels a cool gentle hand on her forehead and words in a friendly voice come to her.

The hut suddenly darkens. The young woman who sits with her back to the entrance, crouching over her work, turns round slowly, turns and gets up, knowing full well who it is standing there blocking the light.

Joel. One of the teachers. Joel who has money and buys gifts. Joel with his sharp eyes and gentle voice. Joel who takes hold of her, Joel with his strong demanding warm body. Who talks about children. Many children, who will belong to him. The young woman in the hut has one. A little child without a father. Sonia hasn't any. She's been pregnant twice. But she hasn't borne a living child. Dead babies. Joel cried over Sonia's dead babies. No man deserves that again and again.

The young woman has said 'Yes' to him.

When she lies on the straw mat at the back of the hut, behind the tattered curtain, she knows she's a real woman. One who gives men living children. With her arms round the neck of the man who will be her husband, she thinks of Sonia, who's in hospital. If she doesn't manage it this time he'll send her away. Joel.

*

Sonia opens her eyes and looks into a big lamp with a hard light. Strange people part her legs. They smile kindly and tell her to breathe calmly.

Better than Yvonne

Julia stands in the shadow just inside the door of the assembly room and looks out at the terrace. Soft golden sunlight on the festive table; white cloth, big plates of cakes and biscuits, tea and coffee, Coca-Cola and Fanta. The guests sit with their backs to her; Julia can study their profiles each time they turn to speak to their neighbours, and they do that constantly, talk and talk in loud, slightly strained voices. The guest of honour is straight in front of her; he's a minister in the government. Julia studies his fat neck that bulges over his shirt collar; he's hung his jacket over the back of his chair. On his left are the American ladies Susan and Phyllis who have come all the way from New York to see how the money contributed by their organization is being spent. The minister is talking to Susan; courteous and excited, he talks to Susan from America. He has one of the seminar leaders on his other side, and next to her is a woman consul from some European country or other; a tall, fair woman with smiling blue eyes, chatting to a group of press representatives on her right: two or three blacks, probably from Radio Kenya, and two whites on the other side of the table. They use a language Julia can't understand; she writes and he takes photographs.

Opposite the minister, opposite Julia in the doorway, are the members of the seminar. Not all of them, there wasn't room, but a good many. The rest are in the assembly room behind Julia, at a little table which has a white cloth too, but no cakes or refreshments, because later in the programme the women in here will go out on the terrace as well, to eat and drink and talk to the guests. But now they're silent. And unseen by the people out- side; except for Julia who stands there in the doorway, watching. Tall and slim, in her best dress with a little mother-of-pearl comb in her hair, she stands observing the visitors with dreamy slanting eyes and her mouth curved in a little half-smile.

Like a queen! The French photographer squats down on the terrace; in his viewfinder he sees the minister gesticulating and showing a mouthful of white teeth, the minister leaning forward to talk to Phyllis, click, he shoots, click, he gets one of the minister appearing to take a bite of the seminar leader's cheek, click, click, that might come in useful some time in the future if the government should show signs of toppling, wonder what the editors of *Le Monde* think of Kenya's present gov- ernment? He doesn't know, is only interested in getting pictures, must ask Simone. . . . He takes a step or two backwards to take in the whole table, a bright festive table against the dark background of the wall beneath the sun-roof, but what's that moving in the doorway? He looks up from his camera; Julia in her lovely long dress, slim and long-legged, almost invisible in the semi-dark- ness back there.

Like a queen, thinks Jaques. Like a queen, he thinks, as he goes back to his seat beside Simone.

Julia from the Tana river. From the village on the other side of the river, the other side of the yellow plains where the elephants trample and the zebra run, the other side of the bush where the lions lie in wait, lie in wait with eyes that shine yellow in the dark, and the beastly hyena kill with their powerful jaws. Julia from the wrong side.

Sometimes she's been in the other village, the one on

the right side; with its fertile fields along the river banks, rice, bananas, maize, with bigger houses than her village, square houses with nicely painted outside walls. But this is her first time in Mombasa. And her first seminar.

It was a woman teacher who suggested they should form a women's group. But she'd had to leave before they had it properly organized. The others had asked Julia to take it on. Why Julia? Because she was unmarried. Childless. Had time.

They had started to sell coconuts. Every week each member brought fifteen nuts to the meeting. They built a little kiosk and took turns to stand there and sell. The profit was to go in the bank. But they found that after they had given the sellers their modest pay there was nothing left for the bank.

They do a little weaving too.

'What have you hit on now?' asks Simone.
'Cleopatra. In the shadow of the doorway. . .'

The seminar leader bids the guests welcome. On the table in front of her a shiny little mike makes a thin metallic squeak when she speaks. She introduces the guest of honour and moves the microphone over to the minister.

He rises. Talks of changes in funding policy for local projects designed to improve living conditions generally. His long sentences are full of words they aren't used to on the other side of the Tana river. Hospitals and wells, for instance, he says in between everything else. New schools and a boat that takes passengers maybe. . . .

A hospital in the little village by the Tana river? Up to now they've managed with dried herbs, scraps of hide and cords round the wrist . . . the old couple at the mission station are the only ones to have talked about a hospital; far away in the country they came from long ago somebody was going to collect money. But no one has seen any of it, anyhow not in the village beyond the plains.

Julia tries to understand the meaning behind the minister's strange long sentences. Does he promise them clinics? Piped water? Doesn't he say they'll get money if they just send in an application?

The minister comes to an end. The seminarists who have been sitting round the table get up and join the others in the assembly room. Giggling and laughing they put on kangas over their dresses; most are yellow, but some are red, grey and white; patterned kangas, with spots, leaves: one has a kanga with a red umbrella on the back. Some fold them in a special way to turn them into little short skirts round their waists or hips.

Then they follow each other out on to the paved terrace in front of the guests; led by Annie from Ngao, all clapping and shouting.

Jaques is entranced as he sits beside Simone and watches the flowing movement of colours and women and rhythms and song. They form a circle. Two go into the middle, and enact a kind of fight; they pick a quarrel, start to fight, try to chase each other out of the circle; Jaques guesses at two squabbling co-wives. He leans across the table, shoots, click, click, gets up and walks round, stands by the wall on the other side of the circle, bends over, click.

Bare feet, gracefully swinging arms, twisting hips. A new dance. A new rhythm. A different story. Jaques takes pictures: of Annie from Ngao; of Eliza from Kwale; Mary from Kilifi. But none of Julia, although it's her he keeps in the corner of his eye the whole time.

Julia, who was the last in the row, towered almost a head above the others, the only one who doesn't go barefoot but wears white shoes with heels. Julia, who goes round with the others, stands in her place in the circle, changes rhythm at the right moment, claps her hands in time with the others. But Jaques knows better; she's not really here, she's quite unaware of what she does, this long-legged girl in her soft brocade dress with an artificial rose on her breast, mother-of-pearl comb in her hair and white shoes with ankle straps. She dreams of something or other behind the wall around the terrace, behind the water below, past the ferry landing on the other side with the dark trees behind. . . .

Jaques photographs Julia. Her tall, feminine form full length; from in front, from the back, the side, as she claps, as she lifts her head still higher and shows her strangely absent manner even more clearly. He takes close-ups of her face, with the narrow eyes at one and the same time veiled and shining, the high cheek bones, straight nose and full rosy mouth with corners that turn up even when she's serious. When he looks up from the camera, Jaques looks everywhere but at Julia, but when he hides behind it he sees only her. He dreams of undressing her. Not as a man but a photographer. He wants to discover all of her, stomach, her hips, her breasts, thighs and knees that hide under brocade and yellow kanga from her waist downwards.

Jaques is in his studio in the rue de Rêves, Paris; he does extra work for the big fashion houses, he has Julia in his spotlight. She's every bit as beautiful as Khadija Adam, last year's Miss Africa, who works for Yves Saint Laurent, and she'll be far better than Yvonne, the snake charmer from the savannahs who is giving Grace Jones a run for her money. Jaques has photographed both of them, now he wants to photograph Julia; no more fishnet and shoulder pads, no more of Khadija's superficial beauty; Jaques is going to create the neo-Romantic movement with the aid of Julia's secret femininity, her shyness, her beautiful dreams. . . .

After the dancing they eat. The seminarists have brought out more chairs to the terrace where they performed so everyone can sit there. Phyllis from New York makes a short speech of greeting.

'You must always remember,' she says, 'that no matter where you come from and what you do; whether you're working on water projects or keep a few goats . . . far across the world on the other side of the ocean someone is thinking about you. All the time. It's Susan and Phyllis. Susan and I think about you. We shall persuade our organizations to support the work still more and we'll come back to see how it goes, don't forget that. . . .'

Jaques watches the expression on Julia's face and guesses she quite agrees with him on how to describe American charity in general and Phyllis from New York in particular. He tries to meet her eyes.

Wonder what it's like in New York? To go by air. . . over Africa; look down on the dry yellow plains, the crocodiles in the Tana river, Mount Kenya, Kilimanjaro, over the blue, green, grey, black sea she's seen pictures of, the sea on the other side, the American sea. . . .

Julia has been in a bus. She has only been in a bus once and that was yesterday, from the road that goes through the village on the right side of the Tana river and on to Mombasa. In a week's time she'll ride in a bus once more, back to her home, with the woman from the women's group in the other village. But when the bus stops the other woman will wave goodbye and go into the house where she lives just beside the road to Mombasa, while Julia, Julia has to cross the river with the crocodiles, walk across the plains, through the bush and back to the other women in the group waiting to hear the story of the seminar.

The formal opening is over. The guests have been given the programme for the week, invited to look around, go into the house and explore the accommodation in the Kikoni YWCA conference centre.

Simone keeps Jaques busy, she wants to go here, go there, hold interviews, see classrooms and dining hall, and Jaques must take pictures. Out of the corner of his eye he sees Julia talking to the journalist from Radio Kenya. Oh, long-legged goddess, will you come to France with me? You can sleep in a silken bed and take a foam bath every day and I will make your face, your legs, your shoulders into this year's face, legs and shoulders. . . . Simone wants a picture of the seminar leaders under a portrait of President Moi.

'From the Tana river. We sell nuts. Coconuts.'

Radio Kenya wants to know the number of members, how long the group has existed. . . .

'Why were you chosen as leader?'

'Because I'm not married. . . .'

'How old are you?'

'Twenty-five. . . .'

'You're twenty-five and not married?'

'I wanted to wait . . . I want to wait till I have some money in the bank. Till I get a job . . . maybe till the group starts to make a profit . . . if I get married and have children and I have some money in the bank it won't matter so much if my husband and I fall out. . . .'

Radio Kenya is a dynamic young man who fires off questions without bothering about the answers; he notes down Julia's words without batting an eyelid, does he take in what she says? Does he notice she's ill at ease: she's not standing there dreaming, she's fully alert, looks hard and wonderingly at the first journalist of her life, at the mouth demanding to know. . . . With a brief word of farewell he leaves her. To the next kanga-clad woman; to hear about other groups in other places, who sell tea, save up for a boat, dream of a baking oven.

Julia walks slowly away from the terrace, round the building and down the sloping lawn. The voices behind her grow fainter; she leans against one of the trees along the edge of the yellow-green slope where it's bounded by a little gravel path; she leans her back against the trunk, bends her head back and closes her eyes. The YWCA, the seminar building in Likoni, Mombasa, journalists, ministers, the other women; they're all a confused mix-up inside her head, Julia doesn't know them, she doesn't even know Annie from Ngao, what on earth is she doing here? An honour, an honour to come here. Go in a bus. Walk along the wide streets. Look in at the restaurants; at people eating food she's never tasted, drinking wines she's never heard the names of. An honour. . . . Oh no, it's no honour for Julia to be group leader, it's an insult to be chosen as leader; Julia, Julia can do it, she's not married, has no children, nothing to do anyway, poor Julia, doesn't anyone want her then. . . .

She opens her eyes. Through the trees she sees the ferry stage, the glittering water; she walks on, crosses the gravel path, takes off her nice white shoes and walks down to the water's edge. She sits on the ground and pulls her knees up, winds her arms round them and gazes at the blue ripples through narrowed eyes. It's different from the Tana river.

Simone has talked to Annie and Mary, to Eliza and Phyllis. She's made a note of the subjects to be discussed in the seminar: Planning; Book-keeping; Questions on eleadership; The ideal number of members; Relations with the authorities.

'Are you ready?' she asks.

Jaques looks around him. Quick sharp glances from group to group on the terrace. He walks with quick steps into the assembly room, on into the kitchen, and ends up in the women's dormitory.

'What do you want? What's the idea?'

Simone has followed him. She wants to go into Mombasa. They have an appointment with Elvina at the Tototo Centre.

Simone thinks about the questions she'll ask Elvina. Questions you can ask a woman you're talking to alone, things you can't ask on an open terrace with people coming and going on all sides; what does she want to know about these women that she doesn't know already?

The ferry is alongside, Simone drives cautiously down the concreted slope and on board.

Jaques runs his long fingers through his thick hair, lights a Gauloise and leans his arm out of the open window. The small deck is packed with cars. A woman stands just beside Jaques eating a brown toasted corncob. A young man in a shabby vest and expressionless face lolls against the side. Two big girls in school uniform lean against the ship's rail and laugh. They glance at the European blowing cigarette smoke out of his window but can't see his eyes; they can only see a pair of shining glasses that reflect themselves, the other cars, the rail, the man in the shabby vest. . . . Jaques' eyes behind the glasses are open but he doesn't see the schoolgirls. He is in Paris, in his studio. He has found a tree, an ashen grey trunk, a green crown filtering light from a spotlight on the ceiling. Julia stands against the trunk, beautiful and long-legged, and looks slightly to the side of the camera's eye with her dreaming eyes.

Julia leans against the trunk, lovely and dreaming; she looks at the water, quite unlike the water in the Tana river at home, and she watches a ferry making fast to the quay far away on the other side.

Green mamba

Eliza, second-in-command of Kibera Weavers. She sits on one stool with her feet up on another, knits with blue wool and offers to show me round the Snake Park and the National Museum, if I haven't been already. On Sunday.

It's only when we meet at the museum entrance that I see she uses crutches, the same kind we have, made of light metal and grey plastic.

First we go to the Snake Park. Eliza goes in front, on light feet down the stone steps. She points to the glass cases with one crutch, delighted; cage after cage of slithering snakes; she laughs aloud and studies my face to see if I'm repelled or frightened. We stand a long time admiring a cageful of splendid green mambas while Eliza talks of the time her brother found one coiled around the engine in his car.

Eliza. In a brown, pleated skirt and green blouse. The story about her brother sounds recent. Isn't she married? Does she live at home?

She goes on talking about snakes after we've been right round the park, when we cross the square to go to the National Museum, while we're studying history.

'Do you know which are the most dangerous?'

We're just inside the door. The wall facing us is hung with old-time weapons. 'Well-known firearms from the past.' We see a 'British tower, flintcoe musket.' And a 'German cavalry carbine.' Beside the weapons is a collection of old East African coins. In the centre are several series stamped with a smiling Queen Elizabeth in profile.

'No?'

'The puff adder. The puff adder is the most dangerous snake. Specially the one that's short and thick like a sausage. If it bites you, in the foot, say, you must cut off your leg at the knee at once; if the blood that's been poisoned gets to the heart you die immediately. But who would always carry a sharp knife with them, and who could manage to cut off their own leg. . . ?'

We're up on the first floor, in the Liberation section. Four walls with black and white photographs. Eliza sits down on a chair by the wall to rest her bad leg. I make the round, from Picture No. 1 onwards, and grow more and more amazed.

'They show more about the white campaign against the Mau Mau than about the black one against the whites,' I say.

'Oh,' says Eliza, 'Do they?'

'Is this the first time you've been here?' I ask.

'Yes. But I've been to the Snake Park lots of times.'

On one of the walls the line of photographs is broken by a large painting that shows an episode from the early twenties: a young woman, heading a silent demonstration, has been mown down and killed. A grim picture with bloody black corpses in the foreground and white violence in the background. The plaque beneath the painting explains almost apologetically that it was this episode that set off the battle for liberation; where was the triumph of victory? African courage? The African heroes?

'My brother took part in the fighting,' says Eliza.

She mentions it briefly, like a statement, not the introduction to further discussion. She gets up, takes a step towards the exit, and I follow her. We stop by the wall charts showing tribal traditions. Several of them picture women or men in full costume and with sharp knives just before a circumcision ceremony. In others we see pale, serious young girls and boys immediately after it. Eliza seems unaffected, she is a Luo and the Luos have never practised circumcision. I've guessed she's a Luo because the middle teeth in her lower jaw are missing; instead of circumcision as a ritual sign of maturity, the Luos have the custom of pulling out their young people's teeth. The origin of this practise is partly to do with the fear of epilepsy.

'Aren't there any snakes in Norway?' she asks.

'Only small ones. We have adders and grass snakes.'

Eliza says I must go back to lunch with her afterwards. I think: so she doesn't live at home then. Does she live alone? Can a single woman who works live alone in Kenya? Of course. Of course she can.

We go through a room filled with stuffed wild animals. See models and jawbone fragments of Dryopithecus, an extinct humanoid ape that earliest finds prove to have lived near Lake Victoria twenty million years ago. We see fashions in dress from the time before the Europeans came and ridiculed men who did not wear trousers. The women were allowed to keep their kangas; they were not so very different from European dresses. We leave the museum and go out to my hired car.

Eliza from Nyanza, born and bred in a village whose name she translates as 'He that you want'. Educated at a mission station, she later learned textile production with financial aid from the missionaries in her village. She lives at Kibera, a few minutes' walk from the weaving room she's shortly to manage. Kibera is a semi-slum district on the outskirts of Nairobi; narrow roads crossing each other, small single-storey houses shoulder to shoulder with each other. Some have fences around them with chickens behind the netting. Others a couple of tethered goats. There are small carpenters' workshops where beds or tables are made. Tinsmiths hammer kettles. Men work at sewing machines. It's hard to find a parking place. Eliza tells me to stop; she ponders, searches the rows of planked and corrugated houses, asks me to drive on. Round a corner there's a small open space with room to park a dented yellow car.

She has two rooms at one end of a house. Heavy blue wooden doors that look as if they came from somewhere else. Two darkish rooms with woven floor and wall coverings, a table with a cloth, benches and chairs with bright-coloured cushions. They are like the students' rooms for girls in Norwegian domestic science colleges. Suddenly the idea strikes me that perhaps a snake injured Eliza's leg. A snake bite in the foot, her brother chopping at her thigh with a knife but not cutting it through . . .

She takes off her smart red scarf and sets about conjuring up chicken and rice and white bread, while she heats water on the jiko, a combined kettle and stove made by the tinsmiths who hammer away in the neighbouring houses.

While we eat she tells me about her leg without being asked.

It happened one summer day in Kisumu. An important building was to be formally opened; it was a gift from Russia to the Kenyan people and Jomo Kenyatta was to head the ceremonial delegation.

'Kenyatta was a Kikuyu. Kisumu is in Nyanza. Luoland.'

Kenyatta's vice-president had been a Luo, and time after time Kenyatta had put various spokes in his wheel. He was to be avenged in Kisumu. When the President arrived, protected by security guards on all sides, a group of Luos had literally put obstacles in his way. He was stopped. It was only a few hundred yards to the destination, where local politicians and representatives from the Soviet Embassy were waiting with architects and others concerned, but the President could not get to them. Women and men and children, come to see the highest authorities in the land, stood on both sides of the road. Even though he was a Kikuyu they had come to clap, even though it was common knowledge that he had obstructed Odingo Odingo more than once, the people of Kisumu had nevertheless come in their glad rags to see a real president. Eliza stood just beside a group of schoolchildren smartly ranged in uniform on the pavement.

But the President did not come. They could see where the cars were; three black cars from Nairobi, but they didn't move; they'd stopped, something in the road prevented them. The schoolchildren had run down there to look. Eliza and some others followed them.

Three furious black cars from Nairobi tried to turn round in the narrow road, put their noses in the direction they'd come from, accelerated with a roar and were off; away from Luo-land, Kisumu and the saboteurs who had blocked their way. And as they roared off they opened fire wildly. Jomo Kenyatta's greeting to the people of Nyanza; fifteen schoolchildren killed and as many wounded. It was a bullet from the President's security men that smashed Eliza's leg.

I've barely digested her story when the door opens and a man comes in. A powerful, tall figure of a man who tears open the door and slams it behind him, a man in semi-darkness with open-necked shirt and a brown knitted cap on his head. He blinks; because of the sudden transition from the light outside to the darkness inside, or because he's unexpectedly caught sight of me, a stranger. Then he snatches off his cap and sits down on a chair.

'This is my husband,' says Eliza. 'He comes here once a month to take all the money I earn off me. It was pay-day yesterday.'

She smiles amiably and speaks to the man in the Luo tongue. He offers me his hand with a slight bow, sizes me up briefly and withdraws his gaze. Eliza gets out another plate and cup and serves him. He eats fast, in silence. She talks to him again, he replies with a grunt.

'He's going back this evening,' says Eliza. 'He usually does that.'

The man understands little or no English; he eats and grunts and sits restlessly on his chair after he's finished.

'He wants money to drink in the bar with,' says Eliza.

I feel like leaving but see that's not possible. I'll go on sitting here in the semi-darkness, at the wooden table with the blue cloth, all afternoon until it's almost time for the bus that goes westwards to leave. Then I'll probably offer to drive the man to the nearest bus stop. I eke out my tea, find my cigarettes and light one. It stikes me I'm not being polite; I offer one to the man, he grabs the packet eagerly and lets me light his cigarette with my lighter. His face grows more open and friendly. Eliza gets up and fetches a big shell for us to use as an ashtray.

'I earn 900 a month,' my hostess tells me. 'I pay 150 to live here. It costs me 100 to keep my son in school, how much d'you think is reasonable for this man to get, for himself and his other wife and mother and father and to fritter away in bars?'

The situation makes me think of Hugo, my blind cousin. Hugo is adult and married, he works in a telephone exchange and is quite independent. But when Hugo and his wife go clothes shopping for him, the shop assistants always ask the same questions over his head: 'Does he like blue? Does he like wide trousers?'

Does he like going to bars? Does he think it's reasonable for Eliza to support both him and his other wife plus parents?

No, the situation is not the same, it's completely different.

'100 shillings, perhaps,' I say.

Eliza nods reluctantly.

'I need 300 for food for myself and the girl. And she needs new shoes too.'

'What girl? Where is she?'

'She's with some neighbours a couple of houses away. She lives with me. The boy's at school somewhere else.'

Eliza reels off more items and adds on sums. She needs to start saving for her daughter's higher education. Then there's that operation she should have had. . . .

'200,' she says. 'He can have 200 shillings.'

Her husband stubs out his cigarette, sits and squeezes the knitted cap between his hands. Eliza opens the bag hanging on her chair, gets out her purse and takes out two 100–shilling notes. She hands them to him across the table. He straightens his back with a jerk, his body seems far too big for the small room, and he looks at the two proffered notes as if he's going to refuse them. Then he looks at her with a dangerous glint in his eye. His whole body tenses under his shirt. His temples shine and glitter.

'He won't touch me while you're here,' Eliza says with her eyes on him, not me. Eye against eye. Stubborn wills formed by a history in which they themselves are infinitely little. A history that makes her eyes twinkle teasingly and keeps him in check. Just for today. I think of what he might have done to her with those strong rough fists of his, two fists at once, two fists with a tight grasp of a coarsely knitted grey-brown cap between thighs quivering under trousers shiny with wear.

For a long minute she holds out the notes over the

table. Two long minutes. A narrow little hand hanging in the air above the dish of chicken-bones, rice and crumbs of white bread, three empty plates and three cups of tea.

Her crutches are propped against the wall behind her. A big round basket of wool is in the corner beside them. A few houses away is a small girl on a visit to the neighbours; at a school far away there's a boy. And I thought she was unmarried. Lonely and unmarried because of her leg. I recall her laughter in the Snake Park, the story of the green mamba in her brother's engine. . . .

The red silk dress

It's a desperately unhappy Alice we find when we've finally managed to ask our way to the right house in the Mathare Valley. She's had a break-in; someone has stolen a radio, a silk dress and a pair of shoes.

On our way here we've discussed *favela* in Brazil and Palestinian refugee camps; my companion was stationed at the embassy in Rio for some years.

'Slums are the same the world over,' my companion said, and: 'If you give them money you must never give more than people can spend in one day; if you give more you can cause death and create murderers.'

We had left the streets of central Nairobi behind us; offices, hotels, the broad avenues and boulevards with more and less well-dressed people, black and white, making their more or less purposeful way towards something or other. The rows of vacant taxis. Car hire firms. Shoe-cleaners. We were on our way out of town. On both sides of the road was scorched dry yellow grass; on one side a slope down to a valley which widened out to provide space for thousands of little huts and shacks; the Mathare Valley, home for 150,000 poor, destitute people who had come to Nairobi from near and far, filled with dreams of work, money, happiness.

Chock-a-block with one-room houses; square huts made of mud, planks, tin sheeting. Beside each other, behind each other, with narrow streets in between them where it's almost impossible for two to walk abreast. Like streets in a camp. Open gutters. A pungent stink of refuse and sewage.

I think: what do these people live on? The place reminds

me of the camps in Beirut, but not entirely. The Palestinians are well organized, they live in quite a different manner, don't they? With schools, kindergartens, hospitals they run themselves in the camps, at least until they were bombed to bits; and work, before the war many of them at least had steady jobs in Lebanese factories. . . .

'It was impossible to go out at night in Rio,' my companion says. 'The wife of a friend of mine was almost strangled by someone who grabbed the chain she wore around her neck. . . .'

Now and again there are small open spaces in front of the houses. Half-naked children. Flies. Snot. Many of them are handicapped. Men stand along the walls; idle, hands in pockets, a cold stub in their fists. When we ask them for Alice's house they shrug their shoulders or indicate the way with an almost imperceptible nod.

At last we're there. We have acquired quite a tail of children behind us; inquisitive and serious. Outside Alice's hut they join her own three, and one that belongs to her sister.

Alice is alone in there in the dark. A bundle on the bed at the back of the room. She gets up slowly, tries to smile without success.

'If you just leave anything for a second they steal it. . . .'

'What have they stolen?'

'The radio. And my dress. And a pair of shoes.'

'Who steals things?'

'Anyone and everyone. The next door neighbour come to that.'

We begin to get used to the darkness of the hut; glimpse the bed, a high wooden bed with a frame round it. Do both women and all the children sleep in the one bed? Do they have husbands as well?

All I know about Alice and the other woman is what my

companion told me on the way here: he pays for her sister to go to school. He met her by chance some months ago as he was coming out of a cinema. He was alone and the last to leave. Maybe he stopped to look at the pictures. Maybe he stood still for a few moments to light up. He smokes the whole time, little thin cigarillos. Anyway he caught sight of the young girl in a thin summer dress standing by the wall, looking at him despairingly. So he started to talk to her. And she told him the story of how she and her sister had been driven away from home into the town to fend for themselves. Her sister had sent her out to earn money: it was the first time, would he like her body?

Erik Henriksen, a minor official at the Norwegian embassy, engaged to a girl studying forestry at the agricultural college in Ås, missing and longing for Marianne from Våga, had he stood there under the African neon and moonlight and swallowed or not swallowed, fought an inner battle with himself or not? How should I know? I don't know him. I only saw his profile while he talked about it, in a voice that was different from when it was describing the slums of Rio, San Paulo, Sao Luis; a slightly breathless voice that told of a girl he had helped send to school, to whom he gave money every month in return for her promise that she wouldn't go on the street but sit at a desk and learn, so that she could be something. Something else.

'Is Margaret at school?'

Alice shakes her head.

'Where is she?'

'In town. At the doctor's.'

'Is she ill?'

Alice nods.

'Is it serious?'

Alice shrugs her shoulders.

She gets up and shouts something to the children bunched together in the narrow alleyway between this and the next house. A boy of about six puts his head in the doorway. Alice gives him some coins and he vanishes.

Erik lights a cigarillo. I look around me at the house: a low wooden bench, two stools and a small table. On the floor there's a yellow washing-up bowl full of dirty cups and pots. A jiko, combined stove and kettle. I squash a mosquito that's biting my arm and get my fingers covered with blood. I throw a glance at Alice. A plump well-built girl in her twenties, small heart-shaped face, receding chin and sloping front teeth. Her hair is hidden under a scarf. Large breasts under a dress with shoulder straps. One of the straps has fallen down and hangs loosely around her upper arm.

'When did you get the radio?' asks Erik.

'A few weeks ago.'

The little boy comes back with two bottles of Fanta, one for Erik and one for me. I ask if Alice or the children are having a drink too, and she laughs and says no. Drinks are for guests. Ice-cold Fanta straight from the bottle. The children gaze at us from the doorway.

'How's Margaret getting on at school?' asks Erik.

'She hasn't been for the last few days.'

'Because she's ill?'

'No. Because she can't afford to buy new books. The teacher says there's no point in going to school if she doesn't have the books. . . .'

Erik lights a new cigarillo. He puts his empty bottle on the table. He gets out his wallet and takes out three 100–shilling notes. He thumbs through them slowly and laboriously, looks carefully at them before he hands them to Alice, who accepts without looking at them, as if they were made of air, invisible, unimportant, unreal. Then, as if by magic, they've gone; under her on the stool, hidden among her clothes. . . . On the wall behind her hangs a page from a magazine; a colour photo of the coast, an advert for a hotel or travel agent; sunburned white people in deckchairs beside a swimming pool. Palms in the background. I ask where the sisters come from. Erik answers. He utters a name I haven't heard before. Then explains further: it's inland. On the way to Kisumu. Same tribe as President Moi. Kalendjin. The same tribe as Kip Keino and Henry Kono, have I heard of it? Yes, I remember, was it from the Olympic Games in 1972? I remember it well, it was the only time I had sat there hour after hour, day after day, watching event after event. I was heavily pregnant, past my time; I half-sat and half-lay on a sofa eating bar after bar of milk chocolate. . . . Alice shrugs her shoulders. At my thoughts. Or at the President and Kip Keino. I ask Erik if we can leave soon. He lights yet another cigarillo and gets up.

I see her in my mind's eye as I sit on the terrace of the Boulevard Hotel the same evening. Shrugging her shoulders. The strap that hung round the soft plump upper arm. The notes that vanished. I think of the wall in Rio de Janeiro that divides the poor quarters from the western part of the town. The peeling walls and glassless windows of the black quarter in New York. The Palestinian refugees who instead of stealing share all that they have because they are a united people, one idea, one dream, and not a conglomerate of human beings with different religions, different histories and tribal traditions. I drink Campari and admire the flowers in the aquarium on the terrace in front of me. Blue flowers. Red. With beautiful big petals swaying a few inches above the water with threadlike stalks in the goldfish forest in the glass case. At the neighbouring tables sit black women and European men. The women are beautifully dressed, in silver trews, high-heeled shoes, evening dresses. At the table nearest me, a smiling woman in her twenties in talking to an Englishman. She wears gold shoes and a dress of soft red silk. I empty my glass and leave.

Black crows

This is my last day in Africa. I stand on the shore of the Indian Ocean, and tomorrow I'll be on my way home. Since I landed at Nairobi airport three weeks ago I've been on duty full time as my own secretary-receptionist, I've filled page after page between the silk-embroidered covers of my Chinese notebook with neat and tidy accounts of acacias and flamboyants, women's lives filled with children, market-places crammed with baskets, rugs, drums, stringed instruments, fruit, cripples, pictures scored on slabs of dried banana skins, but at last the secretary has been dismissed, and it's I myself standing on the shore of this Indian Ocean, barefoot on the warm yellow-white sand, I wading into the water, swimming out through the warm breakers, lying on my back looking up at a blue, blue sky I may never see again.

It's I myself walking up again, past the guard in yellow shorts sitting in the shade of a tree, taking care no tourists are eaten by sharks; I myself climbing the curved stone stairway up to the hotel garden. It's green and luxuriant, full of trees and shrubs with colourful flowers. It's crossed by narrow intersecting gravel paths, the green lawn dotted with empty white-painted sunbeds made of a light wood I don't recognize and blue hotel towels. It's the end of the day, and the guests have gone in to change for dinner; at one of the hotel restaurants if they haven't ordered a taxi to take them into town in search of some exotic place or other, in the Arabic Old Town, perhaps.

I stand at the top of the steps to let the evening breeze

dry my hair. I rest my hands on the low wall dividing the garden from the slope that goes down to the beach, and my palms turn into rough stone, my body is transparent; open to the wind, the smells from the sea, the flowers, light as a feather yet bound to the grass under my feet, the stone under my hands, the faint line out there dividing sky from sea. Closer in are the underwater reefs that make the waves foam and ripple against invisible mountains. A lizard sits on the wall and looks at me, glittering green and yellow, before it vanishes down a crack. Someone clears their throat quite close to me and I jump.

'I didn't mean to startle you . . .'

It's a man, an African; he must have been standing here longer than I have, held by the same picture of sea and sky, hidden behind a tree a few yards away. Now he's taken a step forward. An African man in light-coloured trousers and a white short-sleeved shirt. His clothes indicate he's neither a gardener nor a waiter, and to combat my own white blush, I give him a friendly smile and a strong impression that I haven't anything in common with the master race who fill the hotel with German and French and Italian loud-voiced chatter. He offers me a cigarette as a sign he understands. I accept it and let him light it for me. I ask if he's staying at the hotel and he says 'Maybe.'

'What does that mean?'

'If I don't go on. "I am the fool. The jester . . ."'

We stay there side by side with our faces towards India. The sun's on its way down behind the trees and our necks, the sea and sky ahead are pale and empty; the tide's going out, and the distant reef reveals a long jagged back. The secretary comes to life and scratches at the inside of my forehead, burning to ask the man what he meant by his last remark, burning to get him in between the silk-embroidered covers, and I have to remind her she's off duty.

'You remind me of my wife,' says the African. 'Can I offer you a drink?'

We walk together towards a small bar at the far end of the garden opposite the main hotel buildings. He suggests vodka and rum on a bed of pineapple and we sit down at a small white-painted wrought-iron table.

He's my own age, perhaps younger. He has a long narrow face; his eyes are melancholy although he smiles a lot. For a long time we sit in silence and watch the sunset. Then he turns towards me.

'I went to the States to study in 1976,' he says. 'In connection with a large aid project. Hydroengineering. Black students from various countries took part. We were to stay for three years and then go home to bore wells, lay pipes, erect pumps. It was an interesting course of study; diagrams, visits to various American waterworks. . . . We were there for three years studying a subject we didn't know what we were to do with. While the American lads were looking forward to finishing and starting work, we went around dreaming of other things; law, economics, film. . . . Do you understand?'

His eyes are intense, his mouth shows a touch of irony, I nod, think I understand.

'Instead of going home I started to study medicine. My scholarship had come to an end, and I kept myself by working at a stree: kitchen in the evening, selling hamburgers and chips for McDonald's.'

The sun has gone. Only a narrow pink strip behind the trees tells where it went down. The palm leaves above our heads rustle softly. A few yards away a family of small monkeys stand and watch us. Lights come on in the little bar; red and yellow like the ones in Tivoli but without the roundabouts, the shooting galleries, and rows of gentle teddy bears.

'Then I met Camilla . . .'

White American Camilla, who falls in love with black George. A relationship with a white American Camilla has never entered his head. For three years he's studied pumps and piping systems, been to the cinema with Gira from Uganda, Mario from Somalia and Robert from Mozambique, or to black discos, danced, drunk a few beers and gone home early. He meets white Camilla at the faculty of medicine; she looks at him over her lecture notes, keeps on looking at him when they start practicals at the same department of the same hospital, looks at him with a flash of blue under the green theatre cap.

Why is he telling me this? Why does he get up from his chair and walk restlessly up and down in front of me? Why does he suddenly bark at me to ask him to order me a dry martini?

'What?'

He stops in front of me with his hands impatiently at his sides and I do as he says, ask for a dry martini. I am Camilla, and the garden a piece of America. George is George, he walks to the next table. Behind his back I see the wondering face of the man in the real bar. Before him is an invisible one where a young African student bends over bottles looking for something unfamiliar to him. A banal story. I myself who am white and a woman, raised in a white Western capital, have no idea either how you mix a dry martini. But I've been given the role of Camilla, and I'm squatting in a stylishly furnished room searching through a pile of records for soft music on the first evening my black friend has come home with me to my parents' house.

George picks up one bottle after another, mumbles Jim Beam, Old Crow, pushes batteries of bottles off the table with a long black arm which ends in the air with fingers spread like birds' feathers, and he changes track and tells me an episode from his hydrology days: all the students stand in a window looking down at the ground in front of the building where an old bag of bones of a black woman is being attacked by black crows, to the students' amusement. He flaps his arms and is woman and crow at the same time. He's clever. He makes me laugh.

He comes back and sits down opposite me.

'Where is Camilla now?' I ask.

'In prison. I'm coming to that.'

I shiver under the damp towel. George notices. He stretches out his hand and strokes my arm; the unexpected touch makes me tremble, his face so close to my own seems ravaged.

'You're cold,' he says.

Then he bends down and gets a garment out of a case I haven't noticed before. A short-sleeved shirt with painted yellow buttons; one side is pink, the other green, and the colours join in a zigzag line down front and back. I hang the towel on a chair back and pull the strange shirt over my head. It's tight-fitting and short. It must be even shorter on him.

'Like a jester,' says George.

The night is dark and warm and magical and filled with white and black impotence. The bartender could turn into a lonely statue behind his counter, the night could go on for all eternity, and George and I could take years over each word, each choice, each movement. His stories of the dry martini, of the engagement party six months later in his in-laws' garden, the fine speech by Camilla's liberal father, senator and professor of archeology, the bitchy comments he reads behind the guests' broad smiles, all those are unimportant now, belong somewhere else, in American films with Audrey Hepburn and Spencer Tracy, not here.

But there's more. More important things. We buy more drinks and light more cigarettes. We blow wispy smoke into the air behind each other and I think that George has probably never joined in with the rebellious students in Nairobi year after year demanding their democratic rights, boycotting lectures and holding up the city-centre traffic by linking arms and marching along the width of the road. Why should I think of that now? I look at George, wonder what happened with Camilla.

We get up and leave. When he sees I'm barefoot he finds a pair of shoes in his bag for me, soft felt ones with pointed toes. We walk across the grass, down the winding steps to the beach; we walk away in the moonlight and he tells me the story of eleven-year-old Pearl in the American hospital who was one of the first known victims of the terrible disease AIDS. In a prosaic medical voice he lists the symptoms, which I know already, followed by a description of the mood in the hospital, where he worked with Camilla, when it was realized that the source of infection was neither needles from drug addicts of either sex nor male homosexuals from Haiti but the bad hygiene common to a number of Central African states. He rattles his black bag and I hear a faint ringing sound.

'Have you been a blood donor?' Camilla had asked. 'And I thought nothing of it. The doctors knew. The nurses knew. The white students knew. I was the only one who didn't know.'

In a low voice he shows me a sharp white morning slashed by the sound of ambulance sirens, three white youngsters and a middle-aged black man in a head-on collision; straight into the theatre with them, George is in the team working to save the black. His head had smashed the windscreen. Half of him rested on the bonnet, pierced with sharp glass splinters. The man's ruined face is of minor importance. He had broken ribs. Glass has cut into one of his lungs. His need for blood is pressing. And the hiss of the assistant surgeon: Let the black trash have black trash blood.

'I didn't get it. I didn't get what he meant. And when Camilla cried and asked if I'd been a blood donor before I went to the States, I didn't understand that either. Blood donor, so what?'

He throws out his arms, drops his bag on the sand, takes hold of my shoulders, so hard it hurts, holds me tightly and whispers the words he spoke to his American loved one in another place, another time.

'I'm going back with you,' she screamed. George screams. 'Going back with you into the bush, to work, work there for the rest of our life. . . .

'She wouldn't sleep with me. She thought I had the disease. She thought I'd infected her.'

We sit down on the cool sand. He drops his head on his knees. I stroke his back; stroke him and stroke him while I watch the floating moonlight glitter out there. The tide is out. I think it might be possible to walk right out to the reef. A flock of birds like flamingoes strut about on thin legs only a few yards away. Don't African birds go to sleep at night? I think.

'I managed to convince her I wasn't infected,' George mumbles between his knees. 'And I told her that though doctors are important the most vital thing is water. Clean water. Wells and pipes.'

Then he describes zealous Camilla writing articles for the papers on Water and Africa, the World Bank and Reagan and smug white Americans who have to drain the blood from poor buggers in other places to save white lives. First in Latin America. Her senator father had been down there himself and seen wasted Indians stretching out their arms for a scrap of food

'Then we were married.'

George gets up. His face is pale and strange in the moonlight; it looks grey, mask-like.

'You should have seen my performance,' he says. 'Not the one I've given tonight, that was mere mimicry, but the real thing, beautiful. . . .'

Suddenly he whirls around like a ball, does a somersault, once, twice, three times, uttering short shrill howls. Then stops, stands before me, tall and straight, flings an imaginary cape around him, bows low and calls:

'Comealong, comealong, comealong, co-o-o-me. . . . Everyone ready? To the history of history, standing outside history. Running after bikes, biking after cars, cars after boats, planes or rockets . . .'

He goes on in his own voice: 'This is my country, isn't it? My Kenya. I'm thirty-two and this is the first time I've been to the sea. Who owns the sand? Who owns this beach?'

We have walked a long way; further than the boundary of the Indian who owns the hotel we started from.

'It probably belongs to another Indian hotelier. Or a Brit. Or an Italian . . . Am I boring you?'

Far away out there the dawning of a new day shimmers faintly. I've not eaten since lunch time yesterday. My plane leaves in a few hours and I've not packed yet.

'But why is Camilla in prison?' I ask.

He sits down on the sand again. Looks at me with big eyes. Looks at the sea. Whispers low:

'Because she killed a man. Shot him in the chest. One of the doctors. He wanted to establish a new bridge between peoples. Not made of blood this time. A kidneys bridge. A heart bridge. Frozen black kidney and lungs, eyes and livers, hearts and brains, get it? We had a great party at her parents', we'd been married three weeks, three weeks and one day. . . .'

The birds like flamingoes fly low over the wide shallows. They cry to each other about small fry, nesting grounds, the cheating tide, I follow them with my gaze, out, out towards the new morning. I close my eyes, feel the heaviness of my body, heavy limbs, helpless palms against the cool sand. A nameless negro from a nameless village, helpless against the American wall, too late he grasps what the white man is saying, too late he realizes what the white woman, who to his great amazement has become his wife, is about to do. Too late.

When I open my eyes again he's gone. Far away over there I see his back, erect in the white shirt, his feet in the beige moccasins step lightly. Soon he's no more than a little dot. Is it true his name was George, or was that merely a name I hit on?

I sit on and see how the sea out there slowly fills with blood. Then I get up and walk back. On my way I pick up the black case that jingles when I shake it. When I reach the hotel's section of beach, the Indian's beach, it is full morning, the sun shines big and yellow over the sea and the black gardeners are at work in the garden, picking up yesterday's rubbish, putting out the white-painted sunbeds neatly beside each other. They laugh when they see me in the jester's shirt and felt shoes.

'Have you stolen his things?' asks the head waiter, already presiding over breakfast in the dining room.

I nod. Sit down at one of the tables as the first guest of the day.

A few hours later I'm in the plane. In my own clothes. Beneath me is Africa. Beneath me is George, on the train to Kisumu. He's starting work on the water project at Lake Victoria.